GW00359363

ATLANTIC BEACH

Susan Graham

MINERVA PRESS
MONTREUX LONDON WASHINGTON

ATLANTIC BEACH
Copyright © Susan Graham 1997

All Rights Reserved

No part of this book may be reproduced in any form,
by photocopying or by any electronic or mechanical means,
including information storage or retrieval systems,
without permission in writing from both the copyright owner
and the publisher of this book.

ISBN 1 86106 155 2

First Published 1997 by
MINERVA PRESS
195 Knightsbridge
London SW7 1RE

Printed in Great Britain by
Antony Rowe Ltd, Chippenham, Wiltshire

ATLANTIC BEACH

For H.C.
May your real-life nightmares
no longer taint your dreams.

Acknowledgement

Fiona Harper and Liz Durant thankfully did all the hard work at Med. school so I didn't have to! As a hopeless dyslexic trying to write this book, I owe a debt of gratitude to my spelling checkers: David Thomas, Helen Thomas and Joan Winney. Any mistakes they may have missed can be put down to sheer volume of work! *Nhtak Oyu!*

Susan Graham July 1996.

Prologue

Maggie came out of the laundry room dusting down her beige uniform.

She might not be able to get rid of the smell of cigarettes, but at least she could remove the evidence of two jam doughnuts. She checked the time on her nurse's watch: only five minutes late; no one would have missed her.

The huge hospital elevator came to a stop on the fourth floor. Maggie stepped out and confidently strutted along the corridor sucking hard on an extra-strong mint. She enjoyed her shifts on 'Gynae'; plenty of middle-aged women recovering from hysterectomies with time on their hands, glad to talk to a genial soul in a nurse's uniform. Maggie had been an auxiliary nurse for just over twenty years. She still felt quite chuffed when people mistook her for a real nurse; once, an old man even called her 'sister'. If only she hadn't been so busy with a husband and four kids, she should have sat that SEN. test years ago. One can learn a great deal in twenty years; she often felt she knew more than all these 'Wet-behind-the ears' medical students, forever shuffling around the wards, trying desperately to look like doctors. If only things had been different.

Sister Newton was in charge of the Gynaecology Ward for the night shift. She was sitting at her desk. Maggie passed a catering trolley and instinctively grabbed a glass vase full of dead flowers which someone else had already collected from a patient's bedside. With her thighs slapping together, she marched up to sister, the vase held high.

"Evening sister."

"Oh, hello Maggie."

Maggie headed for the staff room. There was a sink in there. Now that sister had seen her, that should be good for another fifteen minutes or so.

She opened the door and was startled to see someone sitting in the darkened room. A young man was slouched back in a chair, his head leaning against the wall, his eyes shut, and his mouth drooped open. He looked familiar. And exhausted.

"I'm sorry. I didn't mean to - oh, it's you! Hello me duck!"

The young man slowly opened his eyes and looked at the plump woman who had just smashed through his thoughts. "Hi." His croaky voice was hardly audible.

"What are you doing here? Your mob should have left hours ago. I didn't recognise you without your white coat."

Unable to find a suitable, concise answer, David O'Connor just leant his head back against the wall, shut his eyes, and hoped the plump woman would disappear.

He started to think about his life; one minute he was going to be a father, with a career and marriage to look forward to, the next... well, one out of three wasn't a total disaster. Was it?

In another room off the corridor, Helen Slater slept like a baby.

Her light brown hair flopped over her pretty face, she looked younger than her twenty three years. Even after the trauma of general anaesthesia and not a trace of make-up, she looked calm, attractive and vibrant.

David and Helen had both worked for years to come to this hospital, but not like this; one a patient, the other the patient's ex-lover.

The idea had eventually grown on David: 'It could be quite nice to come home to a wife and kid after a seventy-two hour stint in casualty,' he convinced himself, 'it's not as if we would be short of money. I suppose I would have asked Helen to marry me anyway.. I don't know what love is.. but I guess I could love Helen.'

'Besides,..' his argument was complete, '.. the way they work junior doctors, I'll be too knackered to find anyone else!'

David was satisfied his master plan would work; he would marry Helen, she could have the baby, give up work and stay home to look after his child, and in time he would become a wealthy consultant dermatologist (they don't get called out at night) and life for Dr. and Mrs. David O'Connor would be happy ever after.

Helen, however, had other ideas.

Part One

Chapter One

December 23rd 1979

"You stay here, Helen. We won't be long."

Helen was kneeling on the sofa peering out through the window at the tiny, well-kept garden. She never moved her gaze as her mother spoke.

"Helen! Did you hear me? And get your shoes off Granny's furniture!"

"They're not touching her furniture. Where are you going?" She turned around and saw her mother fastening the last button on her overcoat.

"We have to go to the shops. Why don't you go outside and try and make a snowman?"

Helen looked back through the lounge window at the pathetic dusting of snow. The neat little patch of lawn looked like a sponge cake that had been sprinkled with icing sugar.

"Why can't I come with you?"

"No, Helen. You stay here with Granny please. I have my reasons."

'Ah-ha!' thought Helen, 'must be presents for me!'

Helen had not believed in Father Christmas for nearly two years. Ever since her twin brother, Philip, had spilled the beans. At the time, she was too upset to ask him how he found out. They both decided to keep quiet about the revelation, convinced that their parents would continue to buy them bigger and better presents if the twins thought they were from Santa!

"Philip's not going with you, is he?"

"Yes he is. I'm not leaving you two to fight like cat and dog. Poor Granny has enough trouble coping with ONE of you at a time."

Helen turned her back on her mother and put a defiant shoe on a floral cushion. To her disappointment, it didn't leave a mark.

She could hear the voices of her father and brother in the cramped hallway. Her father was in a bad mood.

"For Christ's sake, boy. Get a move on! The bloody shops will be shut in two hours. What did I do to deserve two brats for the price of one? Come on! Shift your arse."

Philip led the way out of the tiny council house, followed by his mother and his still-grumbling dad.

"These bloody kids don't know they're born! As if they haven't got enough bleedin' toys already!"

"They don't have many toys, Dear. Be fair!"

"They've got a bloody sight more than I had when I was their age!"

Helen followed their progress to the Ford Cortina. He didn't mind spending money on his car. Just his children.

She saw the car drive off, her father still fighting the Christmas spirit, her mother looking miserable, and Philip sitting in the middle of the back seat, leaning forward as if nothing had changed. It hadn't.

Helen was forced to get off the sofa as her Grandmother drew the curtains behind her. Most other houses on the council estate kept their curtains pulled back, even when the lights were on. Each of the terraced houses seemed to have differently patterned net curtains in every window. Helen's Grandmother hated net curtains. Her house was the only house in the street without them. Maybe she couldn't afford them, her neighbours would muse.

"Do you want any help, Granny?" Helen followed her into the poky kitchenette. Although her grandmother was a typical, 'little old lady', she virtually filled the tiny space on her own.

"Don't worry, dear. Go and watch the telly."

As Helen gladly obeyed, her grandmother sighed with relief at being on her own for the first time in two days. She loved her daughter dearly, and her grandchildren. But as she got older, the annual task of 'doing her bit' became a torture. As for Jim, her son-in-law, her early suspicions that he was a bit strange had been dispelled. Now, ten years later, she knew he was a complete bastard.

She leant against the stainless steel sink, gulping a sweet sherry. She thought about ways of suggesting *their* house for Christmas, next year. It was only a street away, and it did have the extra bedroom. As she poured herself another warming sherry, she promised herself she would mention it to her daughter. On her fourth sherry, she began to silently curse the Council for having housed her pregnant, newly married daughter so close by. 'Why couldn't they give her a house in Hemel Hempstead? Why should I be a built-in baby-sitter? Been there! Done that!'

Behind the drawn curtains the winter skies had finally grown too heavy. The huge petals of snow floated down, completely covering the sponge-cake lawn.

By six o'clock the white blanket over the council estate was some four inches thick. Helen was lying on the floor in front of the three-bar electric fire colouring in a Christmas card she had made for her parents. Last year she and Philip had made the *Blue Peter* advent candle creation out of wire coat hangers wrapped with silver tinsel. It was proudly dangling from the hall light fitting. No one had the courage to light the candles. At this rate it would last for years! This year, Helen had already made her mother a very useful pen holder out of a cut-down Fairy Liquid bottle. Her father was getting a car sponge, complete with holder – a cut-down Fairy Liquid bottle, and Granny was going to be delighted with a highly decorated treasure box. Just as well Philip needed a new pair of school shoes last month.

Granny, a little the worse for five Harvey's Bristol Creams, looked at her watch, wondering when to start dinner. The twins usually ate at about six, but should she feed Helen first, and Philip when he got in, as he had obviously been delayed with his parents in the Christmas rush, or make Helen wait? She shuffled to the fridge and took out two pork chops. At least Jim always brought plenty of meat with him. But then he did work in a butcher's shop. With his contribution to the Christmas effort being a cheap, scrawny, unclaimed turkey, Jim felt the rest was down to his wife and mother-in-law. He didn't reckon on lifting a finger until January 2nd.

By seven thirty Helen was feeling as tired as Granny. They sat on the sofa waiting for the start of 'The Morecombe and Wise Show'. Ten minutes later, they were both fast asleep.

*

A pale blue Mark 2 Ford Escort with white painted front doors slowly drove along the deserted roads. Waves of snow had obscured the word 'Police' from each side. The dark winter sky had an eerie yellow glow to it. Both occupants of the car had never seen these roads so quiet. In street after street, the 'Panda' car carved out the only tracks in the virgin snow.

The police car slowly moved along the treacherous roads of the council estate. All the terraced houses looked the same; it was difficult to make out the house numbers. Thick slush made driving very unpleasant.

The 'Panda' car came to a stop outside one of the houses. As the policeman and his female colleague got out of the Ford Escort, they both noticed that the house they were heading for was the only one in the road with its curtains drawn.

*

Helen's mother had died instantly. Her father had died a few hours later, and Philip had hung on, in a coma, for three weeks, until he was finally pronounced brain-dead and his grandmother gave her consent for the life-support machine to be turned off.

The over-turned lorry, full of Christmas trees, had crushed the once-immaculate, yellow Ford Cortina like a cheap toy. Like its occupants, the car was unrecognisable when the articulated lorry was lifted off.

For Helen and her grandmother Christmas never happened.

It was assumed that as the one remaining relative, she would look after Helen. The Council had a family from Bradford ready to move into her parents' house. It was months before Helen plucked up courage to cycle past her old home. She swore she would never do it again.

The return to school was awful. She felt people were talking about her, and laughing at her behind her back. Even the teachers now treated her differently. Helen felt so alone. She never did have many friends, choosing instead her brother's companionship. They almost knew what each other was thinking.

And now he was gone.

Helen turned to her books.

They couldn't talk back. She was hungry to learn. Eager to do better. Always a bright girl, she had never been pushed. Now she pushed herself, determined to be as clever as possible. If she couldn't feel like one of the crowd, then she must be better than them. How could people feel sorry for someone that was better than them? Soon, she was.

Her single-mindedness saw her through her grief. Her grades improved; she lived for school.

To Helen her Granny had always looked like a little old lady. The years following her daughter's death had been unkind. Had it not been for Helen, there would be no point to life itself. She channelled her emotions through her granddaughter.

When other twelve year olds were walking in packs around shopping centres on Saturdays, Helen and her grandmother would be working on a Geography project. When other fourteen year olds were giggling about boys, and comparing spots, Helen and her grandmother would be revising for a Chemistry exam. It had begun as the distraction and commitment they both so desperately needed. It had become an obsession.

On Helen's sixteenth birthday, she announced to her grandmother her intention of becoming a doctor.

They both knew it was unusual for girls from council estates to become doctors. But for Helen, it would be more than a possibility.

It was a dead cert!

*

Five weeks after Helen left for university – as if the job had been completed – her grandmother died in her sleep.

Chapter Two

"You stupid bitch!!" David was beside himself with rage. "You think you're so fucking clever, and you can't even remember to take the fucking pills!"

It wasn't as simple as that, but Helen knew better than to argue with him when he was like this. She asked herself what she was doing telling him at all; she had known he wouldn't want a child. Christ! *She* didn't! Not yet! Not like this! Why did she open her big mouth? Just go off and take care of it!

"...If you think I'm going to be saddled with a brat, you bitch, forget it!" He was pacing up and down the floor of his room like a caged tiger, grabbing at his head with both hands, his fingers digging in until it hurt. "How could you *do* this to me?" His eyes darted around his shabby bedroom until they fell on the pine dresser. He marched over to it and with one swipe of his left arm, he sent everything upon it crashing to the floor like a strike at ten-pin bowling. Books, pens, money and beer cans went flying. The noise and fright made Helen clutch her head in her hands. The news of his baby had unleashed the animal.

David stared at the gasping, scared girl in his room. All he saw was rage. He slowly, silently walked towards her. Helen was even more scared than when the noise was deafening. "You stupid bitch!" he screamed in her ear. Helen turned away and started to walk towards the door. David followed her and swung her round by the shoulder, pushing her against the wall. Although terrified, she stared at him defiantly. That was worse than a slap in the face. David raised his fist in line with her head. So close to making contact, he changed course at the last moment. His clenched fist missed her left ear by inches as it buried itself into the plasterboard wall.

As he nursed his crushed hand, Helen went to the safety of the opened door before speaking. "As if you didn't already get the message, we're through. I don't need hassle like this. You've got a real problem, you jerk. Oh. And don't worry about anything; I've already seen the welfare officer and I'm booked in for two weeks tomorrow. I won't be bothering you anymore."

Two months earlier, Helen had contracted the most awful virus. She put it down to a trip to the Indian restaurant down the road. She had been vomiting for two days and felt dreadful all week. Antibiotics didn't seem to help; nothing stayed down – not even the contraceptive pills.

"Booked in for what?" David had followed her out into the road still holding his shattered hand.

Not giving a second thought to the people at the bus stop, just relieved at being out in the open, Helen shouted back, "An abortion, you idiot!"

Chapter Three

David O'Connor was the most beautiful child. With a mop of thick, black wavy hair, bright blue eyes, and a freckled nose, he could get almost anything out of almost anyone.

Doctor Patrick O'Connor headed a family medical centre on the outskirts of Belfast. He always assumed that his eldest son, Paul, would become a doctor. There had been doctors in the O'Connor family for five generations. If only Paul would stop wasting his time drawing pictures and making things! Painting was for sissies. You can't get a real job painting pretty pictures! Paul was actually very talented. But his gift was wasted on his father. By the time Paul turned twelve Patrick O'Connor admitted defeat; his son would never be a doctor. The only subject Paul had any time for was art. That won't get you into Med. school.

There was always David.

Not as intelligent as his elder brother, at least he had no interest in art. In fact, he had no interest in anything.

When David was ten, and his brother had just turned thirteen, their mother left for New Zealand with Tom Crabtree. Doctor Tom Crabtree.

The affair had gone on for years. Paul and David grew quite fond of Uncle Tom, who often was there when they returned from school. David never understood why they just didn't go and buy a new washing machine. Uncle Tom was forever popping over in the afternoons to fix it. And the vacuum cleaner. And the curtain track in her bedroom. What bad luck that these things always happened when Dad was at the surgery. Thank heavens for Uncle Tom!

The day his father found out about the affair was the last day Paul and David saw their mother. Patrick O'Connor felt disgusted, betrayed, angry – and relieved that it wasn't his friendship with a midwife called Anne that had brought things to a head.

Tom Crabtree was much younger than Doctor O'Connor. He had seemed such a nice chap when he briefly worked at the surgery as a locum. O'Connor was even thinking about offering him a permanent position on staff. Now he was contemplating reporting him to the British Medical Association for misconduct.

As a compromise Doctor O'Connor suggested a practice in New Zealand; he couldn't think of anywhere further away. He didn't think for one moment, that when the chips were down, the young doctor would be interested in being saddled with a dowdy, middle-aged housewife; after all, HE hadn't been. She could now come to her senses and start behaving like a respectable doctor's wife.

Put all this nonsense behind her.

The last the boys heard, Doctor and Mrs. Crabtree had moved to Wellington. She was expecting another baby.

Anne, the midwife, moved into the O'Connor house to look after Paul. She shared his father's bedroom.

Doctor O'Connor decided boarding school would be the best place for David. If he were to become a doctor, he needed to be focused. Boarding school would make sure he worked hard.

He just had to work hard. He just had to become a doctor.

On the first day of term David walked up the grand flagstone steps, swallowing back the painful lump in his throat. O'Connor men did not cry.

His father lectured him on the importance of hard work and good results. He said goodbye, then turned towards the car park.

Through blurry eyes, David watched him walk away, and at that moment wanted nothing more than a great big hug.

"Dad!" he screamed after him.

His father swung round, and walked back to his young son.

"What is it?"

"You forgot to say 'goodbye' properly."

"Sorry David." And with that Patrick O'Connor patted him on the shoulder, and shook his tiny hand.

Chapter Four

Helen walked away from the hospital in a daze. She was carrying an overnight case and the small rucksack she used instead of a handbag. There were no flowers. There was no one to meet her.

She walked the half mile to her bed-sit with her mind completely blank. It was a safety mechanism she had taught herself years ago. If unwelcome thoughts did start to creep in, she quickly began taking measured paces, careful not to tread on the cracks in the pavement.

She used to think her ground floor studio apartment was the envy of her fellow students. As she now stood outside, looking at the shabby, lonely, front door, she would have given anything to trade places with someone, anyone, and share. She had had the chance to share an apartment with two other girls. If only she could be there now...

Helen opened the door into a bright, airy hall. It shouldn't be; she had drawn all the curtains before going in for the abortion, leaving the place in near darkness.

Somewhat concerned, she crept towards the equally well lit kitchen. She bumped into someone in the doorway.

David hadn't yet returned her spare door key.

Helen let out a huge sigh of relief. David smiled awkwardly and side-stepped past her, busying himself with a bunch of carnations. He had used an old Perrier bottle for a vase and placed the sad arrangement on her cluttered mantle shelf. He stood back looking at the flowers, finding it impossible to look Helen in the eye just yet.

"David. What the hell are you doing here? You know this isn't going to work!"

David went back into the kitchen, still without looking at her. "Fancy a cup of tea?"

Helen kicked her shoes off and lay on the sofa. The room looked almost tidy. Too weary to fight, too thirsty to care, she closed her eyes. She was fast asleep when David brought in two mugs of tea.

20

*

For most of the first year at Med. school David hardly knew or
cared that Helen Slater existed. She thought the raven-haired Irish
Hot-Head was the most beautiful man she had ever laid eyes on.
Helen was clearly the most gifted student on her intake. She put it
down to hard work. When the others chose to unwind in the Crown &
Sceptre pub Helen, invariably, was alone in her bed-sit.
Towards the end of the first year, she decided to join the others for
an evening drink. The usual crowd was there already. Helen watched
with slight envy as fellow medical students made complete idiots of
themselves. Their raucous, drunken behaviour was tolerated by the
landlord, sometimes even encouraged. Helen wondered if he would
be quite so understanding had they been long-haired, ear-ringed Art
and Design students! David O'Connor was the class joker. He was
always the source of the funniest gags or the stupidest pranks. Not
known for his skills in Anatomy, he once had the whole class in
hysterics with his ventriloquist act using a mutilated cadaver as his
dummy. It was in such bad taste, but done so well. Helen loved his
freedom, the freedom to act as a clown.
As usual, the loudest laughter revolved around David's table.
Helen sat nearby with two sensible female students; a tiny Chinese
girl, and a strapping lass from Yorkshire. They nursed their half
lagers while the antics on the next table kept them amused.
David O'Connor had just been bought another pint of beer. It was
like feeding peanuts to a performing monkey. He looked up at the
stranger who had placed the full glass in front of him and his face
dissolved into a contagious smile.
Feeling obliged to do something funny in order to justify his free
pint, David lifted the tall glass past his lips and placed it on his head.
It nestled nicely within the thick thatch of black hair. Steadying it
with his right hand, he licked up the spills as they dribbled down his
face. Like a circus act, he slowly took his hand away. Moving from
side to side he tried to keep the glass from falling, its contents sloshing
about like the North Sea in winter. He stood up; the glass remained
upright. It veered to the left. He moved to the left. It steadied. The
whole pub was watching the balancing act. They were laughing and
clapping. The now half-empty glass was quite stable, but David,

always the showman, milked the spectacle for all it was worth. Arms outstretched, eyes looking upwards, he slowly circled the pub floor as clearing spectators cheered him on. Helen enjoyed the cabaret.

She could stare at the blue-eyed Adonis without feeling guilty. Her smiles turned to slight panic as Adonis and the glass started to rush towards her, apparently out of control. The whoops of laughter in the pub grew louder as the crowd realised he was on a collision course with the three girls sitting in the corner.

The glass was lurching at a horrible angle. David was desperately trying to catch up with it. The glass was winning. Unable to get out of her chair fast enough, all Helen could manage was a mouse-like squeak as the cold liquid drenched her from her head down. The glass fell, intact, into her lap, closely followed by David O'Connor who remained on his knees while the crowd erupted, cheering wildly.

David kept his head in her lap for a good few seconds. All eyes were on them. Helen, her hands still up in the air, wanted to cry. She felt such a fool. Humiliated beyond belief. Beer dripping through her light brown hair, an idiot in her lap, and half of London falling about in hoots of laughter at her expense.

Slowly, David lifted his head and looked up at a fuming Helen. His blue eyes were even bluer up close. He stuck his bottom lip right out and turned his head slightly to one side.

"I suppose a quick shag is out of the question?"

*

By the third year Helen Slater and David O'Connor were a pair. He made her laugh. She helped him with his study. She made no demands on him; he was still free to act the fool with his male friends, go to the pub whenever he liked, even go out with other women as long as he was discreet. Helen would always be alone at her bed-sit. He could arrive at eleven at night, either unannounced or four hours late, and she would take him in, sober him up, and let him share her sofa bed. Helen hadn't had much of a life before Med. school. She certainly hadn't had much of a sex life. She enjoyed sex with David, but always felt there should be more.

More romance. More foreplay. More fun.

His idea of romance was a bar meal in The Crown & Sceptre. His idea of foreplay was shaking her awake before mounting her. And his idea of fun was to belch out the alphabet in public. That usually meant five pints and a vindaloo before he could manage a 'W'.

Sober, David was a roguish clown. Almost shy, his good looks and impish grin got him out of a lot of scrapes.

Beer became an important part of his day. He needed it to unwind. He needed it to sleep. He needed it to give him a boost. He needed it to function.

By the time Helen grew aware of his dependence on beer, she was hooked; as hooked on him, as he was on beer. One day he would change. As soon as he became a qualified doctor, he would cut down. He knew he had to change. He just hated the nagging. He had only ever hit her twice, and both times Helen knew she had provoked him. He was very sorry afterwards. Helen knew that. She had pushed him. She had to be patient with him.

Then she discovered she was pregnant.

The one time in her life she really needed him – his support, his love, his understanding – he acted like an animal. At last she couldn't understand why so much of her time and energy had been wasted on this man. A wasted man! A pig of a man! How could she have allowed herself to be drawn to him, like a magnet, time after time? Now she saw him differently: a man capable of breaking her heart and her spirit, and maybe a few bones, given half the chance.

*

The trauma of the last few days, and the dregs of anaesthetic left Helen feeling totally miserable and exhausted.

She saw David sitting on the floor watching TV with the sound right down. A cup of tea had gone cold on the table by her head. She looked at the Perrier bottle on the mantelpiece. The brown-tinged carnations were just like the ones on the tables in the local Indian restaurant. No doubt it was a bunch short today. David noticed Helen stir and got up off the floor. He walked to her, leant down, and stroked her hair away from her face. "Hi, Sleepyhead!"

Helen felt the pull of the magnet.

*

For the next two days, Helen came to terms with the abortion. She stayed put, gaining her strength, regaining her self confidence. The welfare officer had put out a story of a bad cold. Helen didn't want the world to know about the abortion, she could barely face the truth herself. It was coming up to the end of year four. She was due some time off. She needed it.

At six o'clock, David let himself in. "Hi, Hel. How'ya doing?"

Helen, still in a white bathrobe, looked up from the sofa. "Don't you think you should spend some time at your own flat? Trevor will have to give you a rebate on your rent, if you keep this up!"

"Let him!"

"You don't mean that!"

"Why not? Why don't I move in here?"

"No way! Apart from the fact that my lease on this place runs out in two weeks, I don't think we should live together."

"You didn't tell me that. Where will you live next year?"

"Oh I don't know. Kim Su has to find a new place as well, she thought we should share. Something will turn up."

"But something HAS turned up. You can share with me! You know my room is big enough for the two of us. And Trevor is okay as flat-mates go..."

"No, David. I need time to think."

David walked into the kitchen and instinctively opened the fridge. Looking long and hard at a can of Carling Black Label, he reached, instead, for a carton of fresh orange juice. Drinking straight from the spout, he rejoined Helen, knowing she would be impressed.

He sat on the sofa, lifting her feet onto his lap. He gently rubbed her toes with one hand as he held the juice carton to his mouth with the other. "I'm going to have a bath. Fancy popping out for a bite to eat, later?"

"No thanks. You go."

After his bath, David appeared wearing old track pants and a torn T-shirt.

"Are you going out like that?"

"I'm not going out. I'm staying here to look after you!"

"You don't have to. I'm fine."

He bent down and kissed her on the lips. That was final. David brought in a tray of leftovers, cheese and bread.

She watched him fill his mouth like a hamster. She picked at some cheese. If he could stay like this forever, she thought, he would make someone a wonderful husband. She drifted off to sleep. David cleared away the tray, covered her with a duvet, and let himself out of the front door as silently as possible.

If he hurried, he might just make last orders at The Crown & Sceptre.

*

Time was a great healer.

During the two weeks before the abortion, Helen had not seen David, except for the occasional glance across a crowded training ward, when neither was prepared, nor able, to say anything. Helen shut her mind to everything other than her studies. David fumed: angry at the news, disgusted by his outbursts, frustrated at the outcome.

It wouldn't have been so bad. Helen was a good sort. Why did she react so violently? Surely she could understand David was shocked by the news? He didn't mean to hit her, or frighten her. What was the matter with her? Couldn't she find it in her to forgive him? David had had two weeks to think things out.

When he went to her bed-sit, the day she was due out of hospital, he knew they were right for each other.

He just had to convince Helen!

Helen had finally raised the courage to ask David for her spare door key; this free and easy come-as-you-like approach was far too threatening for her liking. Sure, he had made a real effort since the abortion, but was it good enough? Could it last? Could a leopard change its spots? She had grave doubts. One step at a time.

In just over a week Helen had some leave due. She strutted along her street, head held high, chuffed at her performance that afternoon with Professor Wilding. Her end of year assessment, postponed due to the abortion, had gone extremely well. In one hour flat, Professor Wilding had given her back a purpose in life, lifted her spirits and proved what a good doctor she was about to make. Nothing could dampen her happiness.

David O'Connor was sitting on her doorstep.

"David. Please! I need some space." She clambered over his legs and unlocked the door.

"I know you do. That's why I'm here." He followed her in. She dropped her rucksack onto the sofa and went about her business as if she were alone. David shadowed her. He had a lot to say, and nothing was coming out.

Finally, irritated by his fussing, Helen gave him centre stage. "Okay, what do you want?"

"Look. You know I'm really sorry for everything. I can't tell you how sorry I am. But I can make it up to you. I swear."

Helen was looking at him with her arms crossed; he sensed her impatience. He went on: "We've got the same leave. A bit of luck, eh?" Helen didn't flinch. "Anyway, I want to make it up to you. Please let me." He took a paper folder out of his jeans back pocket, and gave it to Helen.

"What is it?" She held it limply in her outstretched arm.

"Airline tickets. We're going to the States!"

"Wait a minute! You can't do that!"

"Why not? My father gave me some cash when I started university. I told you I want to make it up to you."

"But I can't afford it. I am so broke, I'm in half!"

"It's on me. Please. I want to."

Helen wondered if the leopard was changing his spots before her very eyes. "We can't do this, David. I just can't!"

Part Two

Chapter Five

Helen walked onto the Boeing 747 first. The cheerful stewardess looked at her boarding card and pointed the way down to the rear of the aircraft. David was close behind, struggling with passports in one hand, their jackets in the other, his boarding card between his teeth, and a small rucksack over his shoulder.

He was quite flushed in the face by the time he reached Helen, having to pass a million people, all with enormous bags which they were trying to squeeze into the overhead bins.

'Why on earth do they bring so much stuff on board with them?' David was thinking as he tugged his bulging rucksack through two fat women, both wearing velour tracksuits, who had clogged up the aisle.

He sat down next to Helen. She looked composed and relaxed. This was her first time on a plane. She thought she would be nervous. When the giant Rolls Royce engines finally roared into action, she was. Terrified, but excited, she peered past the man in the window seat as they were all gently transported into the murky skies above Heathrow. David, a seasoned traveller, having spent most of the summers of his teenage years on holiday in southern Spain, with his father and brother, was quite happy to read the in-flight magazine and menu.

Two hours into the eight hour flight, Helen was a lot calmer. The two quarter bottles of sparkling wine from the drinks trolley had gone straight to her cheeks. She felt very light-hearted. Without thinking of reasons, she outstretched her hand and rested it on David's. He responded by gently squeezing it with his other hand. No words were spoken. They didn't look at each other. They hadn't made love for weeks. Helen wanted it that way. This was the first show of affection by her since she had broken the news of the baby. She had thought it was all over between them. And here they were, sitting hand in hand on a jumbo jet.

Dinner was an experience. Helen was ravenous by the time the neatly packed tray was placed in front of her. As she tried to get to her meal, wrappers, paper napkins, sachets and foil exploded out of the once tidy tray. Pinned between two big men, Helen coped rather well with the tiny knife and fork. She held the child-size utensils up in the air and smiled at David, "What do you think, surgeon's hands, or what?"

After the meal the lights were dimmed, and they were both soon fast asleep. Helen so wanted to watch the movie, but she never made it past the opening credits.

"Ladies and gentlemen, we shall shortly begin our descent into Dulles International Airport, Washington ."

As the enormous aircraft lurched towards the ground, Helen was sure she was witnessing one of the most amazing experiences of her life.

So far.

Following the herd of people through to passport control, Helen worried that her rushed application for a passport was now about to let her down. When she saw the huge black immigration officer beckoning her from the red line, she was sure something had to be wrong. He looked so intimidating in a crisp, perfect uniform showing up hard iron lines in the pure white shirt. His badge was gold, his hair was clipped to within a millimetre of his head, and when he said, "Next," she thought she would faint.

Of course there was no problem, and they soon met up with their luggage.

Helen stood guard by the cart while David negotiated for a rental car.

"It's a white 'Geo Metro', whatever that is." He was reading the details off the key ring. "It was ever so cheap. I hope it's going to be alright."

They walked out into the hot sunshine of late afternoon. The noise of cars and people, busy with their own lives, added to the excitement. The rental car bays were a short walk from the arrivals terminal. As promised, in the middle of a long line of similar cars, was the tiny Metro. Its new white paintwork glistened in the sunlight.

David loaded up the back of the car with the two nylon kit bags, their jackets draped over the top. "I don't think we'll be needing these!" He wiped a trace of sweat from his forehead.

She studied the local map which the girl at the Alamo counter had given to David. He tried to get familiar with being on the wrong side of the car.

As they drove out of the airport Helen had two maps open on her lap. David really needed local directions to get him onto the right highway. Helen was too engrossed with the map of the United States. As David was getting totally confused with the fast moving traffic, Helen was getting more excited with every new sighting of a well-known city on her map. "For God's sake, Helen, which way?"

"Oh I don't know. But Florida's only eight inches away!"

The 267 Expressway into the city was lined with trees. The sprawling concrete road and manicured grass verges were totally free of litter. Everywhere looked clean, green and orderly. David's previous impression of America had been moulded by umpteen low-budget, third-rate, violent films; after seven years locked away at boarding school, the freedom to do what he liked had seemed irresistible. A night at the pub followed by a visit to the video shop, became the pattern of his first year at university. Now, actually in America, he was expecting filth, crime and violence, just like in the movies. He was a little disappointed. Still, there was always a chance the motel rooms would be mildewed and cockroach infested.

The white Geo Metro crossed The Potomac River at Arlington. They followed signs for downtown. Trees and grass turned to concrete and glass. Hordes of people were waiting to cross every street. The little car was dwarfed by buses, trucks and Cadillacs.

"I don't think we'll find a cheap motel here, David."

"I can see that. Okay, we'll just have to spoil ourselves for the first couple of nights. We don't come to Washington every day. What's the name of this road?"

"Er. 9th Street."

"How about this hotel coming up on the right?" Before Helen had a chance to spot it amongst the rows of high-rise grey buildings all around her, David had already turned into the car park entrance of The Renaissance Hotel.

Helen felt totally out of place walking through the foyer. With its highly polished marble floor, elaborate furniture, and uniformed bell-hops, she didn't blend in with the smart people who were milling about. Were they looking at her creased, sweaty jeans? Did they guess she was poor? She felt like announcing, "It's alright, I'm a doctor. Well, nearly".

When she saw the room, she threw herself on the huge, king-size bed. "Oh David, it's wonderful!"

"It should be. We could have got two weeks at a cheap motel for the cost of two nights here!"

Helen looked up at him with a wry smile, as if to say, "shut up and come and screw me."

They made love on top of the bed, items of clothing flung to all corners of the deluxe double room with ensuite facilities.

The cool air mingled with beads of sweat trickling down David's chest. His hard, eager body was on hers. They both felt a sense of urgency and raw lust. It had been a long time, after all. Sex was like a release; from the traffic, noise, crowds, and heat.

As soon as it had begun, it was over.

Chapter Six

They lay, stark naked, on the rumpled bedspread. David dozed off and woke a few minutes later, freezing cold. He got up and turned the AC dial on the wall until the noise stopped. Helen grabbed a handful of bedspread, and covering herself with it, turned on her side and gave into the desire to sleep. She had never experienced jet-lag before. The excitement had kept them on a high so far, but now they could not keep their eyes open. They slept for twelve hours.

It was Helen who woke up first. For a moment she forgot where she was and what she was doing there. Her wave of panic was over when she saw David's naked body next to her, and remembered last night, and the hotel room, and Washington.

After a shower, and a tidy-up, they left on foot to see the U.S. capital.

David picked up a city map from the tourist desk in the foyer and they headed off along H St. towards The White House.

It was more impressive than either of them could have imagined. They walked over to The Ellipse and decided to get tickets for the city tour bus. From the open air carriages they saw Washington: first the Washington Monument, and then, snaking around the city, the sights of The Lincoln Memorial, the Smithsonian, Capitol Hill and Arlington Cemetery were brought within touching distance. They could not decide where to get off and what to see first – they wanted to see it all. Helen had to go to The National Gallery of Art, David wanted to see The Air and Space Museum. They did it all.

The sight of *The Spirit of St. Louis*, *Bell Ranger*, and *Apollo 11*, all in the same enormous room, left David speechless. At The National Gallery of Art, Helen was overcome with emotion when she saw Monet's '*The Japanese Footbridge*'. She had a print of it on the wall of her flat in London, and here she was, two feet from the original! She gave a fleeting thought to her print, rolled up and packed away with all her other worldly possessions in a couple of packing cases in David's flat-mate's cupboard. 'I hope he looks after my stuff.' She smiled to herself when she remembered all the rubbish she owned. Her smile disappeared at the thought of searching for a new flat as soon as she got home. She wasn't ready to share with David; she needed her independence.

By five in the evening they were exhausted. What a day it had been.

Too tired to eat dinner out, they bought a couple of Big Macs and cokes, to go, and strolled back to the hotel.

There was no sex tonight. They fell into bed, and slept until ten o'clock the next morning.

They checked out of The Renaissance five minutes before check out time. David was getting his money's worth. At least he had a rucksack full of mini shampoo and bubble bath bottles, two pens and a writing pad. Even the shower hat and nail file might come in handy one day. Helen had secretly removed the ashtray and bath towel; she didn't think a conviction for theft would look good on his C.V.

They left Washington taking Interstate 95 South.

As loud and busy as the city was, twenty minutes of freeway driving brought them into open countryside. Mile after mile of uncluttered concrete roads, acres of trees and fields, and a very occasional farm building dotted here and there.

The weather was still glorious; not a cloud in the pale blue sky. David pressed the 'seek' button on the radio. When he heard something he liked he pressed it again and settled back. The rock music boomed out of the tiny speakers making the doors rattle. David drove along with a huge grin on his face. It had that effect on him. Not quite Helen's choice, it at least made her happy to see him so relaxed and contented. Hit after hit from the seventies and eighties followed. The miles were just swallowed up.

They had made good progress by lunchtime. Just as they started to feel quite hungry David spotted a roadside café. There were several trucks in the car park. Lots of people were inside, eating. Next door was a small grocery store. A sleepy Alsatian was lying on the wooden verandah outside the shop. An old man was sitting next to him, gently rocking in a rickety old chair. He was wearing saggy denim overalls over a white T-shirt, and a red baseball cap perched high on his head. He was chewing with his mouth open, and nodded slightly as David and Helen walked past him to the restaurant. David smiled. Helen was too busy keeping an eye on the huge dog. The dog ignored her, but raised its snout into David's crotch, wanting to be patted.

The café was basic, but clean. There was one ceiling fan. All the tables under it were full with big, muscular truckers with hairy arms. Helen led the way to a table by the window. David saw all the truckers follow her with their eyes. They ignored him.

A bowl of chilli and a couple of beers later, they were ready to resume their journey. Helen felt quite brave walking past the dog again. From the grocery store they bought a few packets of potato chips, some apples and a six pack of Miller beer. "Is that going to be enough to drink? It's ever so hot!"

"Yeah. You're right." Helen went back for a gigantic bottle of Diet Coke. David went back for another six pack.

When he finished serving them, the old man hobbled back to his rickety old chair.

The sun soon started to fall behind the endless rows of trees. The temperature was still in the nineties. The heat, lunchtime beer, and remains of jet lag were making them both very drowsy. Early night tonight.

By five thirty they started to look out for motels. Once across the Virginia border, they settled on a Days Inn motel just outside Roanoke Rapids.

Their first night in North Carolina.

Chapter Seven

They were out of the motel by 9:30 a.m. and in MacDonald's for breakfast by ten. David was studying the big scale map, seeing where they had been, and where they could get to today.

"Look! There's Cape Fear. I wonder if it's the same one that was in the movie, you know, with Robert De Niro as the weird convict?"

Helen swivelled the map towards her to take a look.

"Robert Mitchum, wasn't it?"

David looked at her blankly, sliding the map back in front of him. Helen went on: "That sounds horrible. I wouldn't mind going to the beach, though. Maybe we could make that our base for a few days. What do you think?"

David thought it was a great idea.

"Well, if Cape Fear is out, which beach?" he said, pushing the map back to Helen.

She studied it while sipping her coffee. Then, as if finding the elusive jigsaw piece, she shouted, "Got it!" and pressed her finger down hard on the map. "Atlantic Beach! Sounds good, doesn't it?"

David nudged her finger to see where she was pointing, and while they finished their coffee he made a mental note of the route they must take to get to Atlantic Beach.

*

It took them the best part of the day to get as far as New Bern. They were still nowhere near the coast. It was early evening when they drove through Morehead City. The smell of the sea finally filtered into the car.

Half way across the iron bridge that spanned Bogue Sound, Helen saw a dolphin frolicking in the calm water. "Oh, my God! It's a shark!"

David had trouble spotting it while he drove, but even with snatched glances through the metal girders of the bridge, he could see it was a dolphin. He smiled to himself. "Don't be stupid. That's Flipper!"

As Helen had seen neither in real life before, shark or dolphin, it had made her day.

Turning right just after the bridge, the spit of land that they were now on looked much bigger than it did on the map. They were obviously here; straight ahead of them was an enormous light blue water tower. The words 'Atlantic Beach', underlined with a dark blue wave pattern, encircled the top of the tower. Beyond it was the Atlantic Ocean.

David turned onto Fort Macon Road. It was a long, straight road, in the heart of Atlantic Beach, lined with restaurants, shops and motels. The sidewalks were busy with people. Most of them seemed to be on vacation. Even the police station looked 'closed for the holidays'. As they drove along the busy main road, the restaurants, shops and motels got smaller and more spaced out. David hoped that meant they would also be cheaper. "Which motel shall we try?"

"Ooh. David. Did you see that one back there that looked like a pirates' ship? It would be very handy for all the shops and restaurants."

"Mmmm. I don't know. This one looks pretty good." They were almost out of the town by now. David turned left into the car park of The Sundowner Motel. It was a drab, grey, two storey building, with paint peeling off the window frames. In the corner of the car park, in full view of the road, was a tiny splash pool with half a dozen sunloungers around it.

Helen noticed the pile of black garbage bags by the entrance to the reception office. Dogs, or something, had obviously got to them, leaving a trail of havoc. David only noticed the sign above the door: 'Vacancy: $34 per room, per night'. "This'll be perfect!"

David checked in with the old boy in the office, and told him he would be needing the room for about a week. He came out to the car with two keys for room seventeen. It was at the end of the first, grey block, on the ground floor. He parked the car in the bay outside their room, and they took everything in with them. The room was spacious and clean, with an air conditioner rattling away under the window. An ancient TV was screwed to the melamine cabinet, and the bed felt like it had a mattress made of sponge. All the walls were covered in a fake dark wood veneer and the heavy curtains looked similar to the ones in Helen's old school hall. But the bathroom was clean. There were no cockroaches. And only a hint of mildew.

"He didn't even want a deposit!" David hung their jackets up in the wardrobe, "They're so trusting. Not a bad price either, given its location."

Helen, still on cloud nine thinking about 'Jaws', was trying out the mattress, by bouncing up and down. David guessed what was to follow, and just had time to draw the musty curtains before a hand came up between his thighs and pulled him onto the bed.

It was nine o'clock by the time they had showered and changed. Helen had stood her ground at the mention of another night in with potato chips and apples for dinner. They set off on foot to explore the immediate area, and to find somewhere to eat.

As the light dimmed, in late evening, the motel looked better. It was nestled amongst sand dunes that led to a stretch of white beach. They walked hand-in-hand along the boardwalk. It was still quite crowded. A couple of beach side kiosks were still open for burgers and hot dogs. Helen kept a tight grip of David's hand as they walked past. The familiar sound of Eric Clapton made David look up. It was coming from a wooden building. Huge wooden posts held up a balcony above their heads. Eric Clapton was sharing the soundwaves with people who were laughing and talking, sitting on the balcony.

"Fancy dinner up there?" David was already tugging her hand towards the wooden steps on the other side of the building. The steps led up to the main entrance door. Above it was a hand painted sign that read: 'Leon's Beach Hut Restaurant'. David walked up while Helen cast her eyes over the menu which was in a glass case on the wall. The small restaurant had a bar on one side, six tables covered with red and white check cloths and a candle on each, and three ceiling fans, which still weren't enough. All the tables were occupied. They sat at the one remaining table, outside on the balcony. The view was magnificent; a white sandy beach, then ocean for as far as the eye could see. On the boardwalk below, couples and families strolled by as the sky over the water turned magenta.

The heavily pregnant waitress gave them each a menu, and came back with two cold beers while they decided.

David's eyes focused on her enormous belly.

An emotional lump came up in his throat which he quickly washed away with the silky smooth beer.

He was not sad at the thought of his baby.

He was very, very angry.

Chapter Eight

When Helen awoke, she was all alone. The little white car was not outside their motel room, and there was no sign of David anywhere. His wallet and car keys were not on the bedside table, where he has put them before going to bed.

She remembered the meal last night: David had been very quiet, actually, she thought he was a pain in the neck. In such a romantic setting, with terrific views and food, he turned all grumpy. 'Could it still be jet lag, I wonder, or maybe that pregnant waitress got to him.' Helen had noticed her bulge as well, and had a fleeting thought of what state of pregnancy she would have been at by now, but quickly put it out of her mind. 'There is no way, I could have had it. End of story!' She was hoping her thoughts were the same as David's. Wherever he was, whatever he was doing. 'Oh God, where is he? Maybe I should have seen more of him before the abortion? Let him come to the hospital with me...but then he may well have talked me out of it.' Her thoughts were fighting with each other. 'He hated the idea of the baby more than I did! Didn't he? ..But then why was he upset when I went in for the abortion? How could he change just like that?' She was sitting on the edge of the bed, deep in thought.

'Oh it's *so* easy for men. *He* didn't have to give up his career! *He* didn't have to go to hospital to have it ripped from his insides!' She was close to tears as her thoughts worked her up to a frenzy.

'I knew I shouldn't have let him back into my life. Bastard! Fancy telling me he came to the hospital, but he was too late. Too late! It was *my* body, *my* baby. How dare he think he could dictate my life for me. I don't even *like* him anymore!!'

As at all other times of stress, she frantically paced around the motel room searching for something to read. Anything. It always helped her to calm down and take her mind off the problem.

She strutted into the bathroom, still seething from her rambling thoughts, carrying a very new looking copy of *The Gideon Bible*.

She had barely finished reading the inscription on the inside front page when she heard the motel door being opened with a key. Slowly, she opened the bathroom door and peered through the crack.

She saw David walk in. He was holding two lidded cups of coffee and a couple of Danish pastries.

Chapter Nine

"Oh. Hello, Helen. You're up."

Helen calmly walked out of the bathroom and slipped the bible back on the shelf under her bedside table.

"Where have you been?" She tried to sound casual.

"Oh. I couldn't sleep so I went for a long walk on the beach. There was no point waking you. Oh. And then I drove to that store by the traffic lights. That's where these came from." He raised a Danish pastry then took a bite out of it.

Helen joined him at the table and they ate breakfast in silence.

"It's a beautiful day, let's just stay on the beach, shall we?" Helen was already tugging her black bathing costume out of her nylon kitbag as she asked him.

"If you want to," he said.

"Well, do YOU want to?"

"I don't mind."

Helen could sense a major mood brewing. David often had these, and she usually ignored him for a couple of days until it blew over. But each day was valuable. This was the holiday of a lifetime. She was not going to let his irrational behaviour spoil both their fun. She tossed her costume onto the bed, then went over to his kitbag and rummaged around until his red swimming shorts appeared. "Come on, let's have those pants off you!" And she pulled at his jogging pants trying to get him to lighten up. It was not the thing to do.

David ground his teeth, and raised his hand ready to hit her, but at the last second, thought better of it. Helen backed right off, and dropped his shorts on the floor by his feet. Silently, she took her costume into the bathroom, locked the door, and changed into it.

"I'll be on the beach if you want to join me." She put a few things into her small rucksack, stuck her sunglasses in her hair, grabbed one of the motel keys, and walked out of the room without giving him a second glance.

She walked through the motel grounds towards the sand dunes, the lapping of waves getting louder all the time. A path made of well-seasoned wooden boards led her through the dunes, straight onto the clean, white sand. The beach stretched for miles either side of her. There were quite a few people, but the beach was so extensive there was plenty of space for everyone to spread out. Helen walked barefoot through the sand towards a grass-covered dune. Taking her T-shirt off and laying it on the flat sand, she was able to lean back on the sand dune. She had brought a book to read, but it was more entertaining to just watch the world go by. Two little children played with buckets and spades in the wet sand while their parents sunbathed. Endless numbers of joggers and walkers went by. Far in the distance, she would see a dark 'V' in the sky, and as it grew bigger, she could make out a flock of pelicans flying along the shoreline. Occasionally, they would drop low, just skimming the surface of the very calm sea, and sometimes they would rise high to a point, and then dive-bomb the unsuspecting fish below.

The gentle rhythm of the tiny waves was too inviting to pass up. She walked down to the water's edge. It was colder than she had hoped. But soon the water was lapping above her knees, and before she knew it, she plunged forward and swam out. Looking back at the beach she could see the wooden balcony of last night's restaurant. People were already sitting out there. Surely it was not lunchtime already.

Her eyes scanned the beach right in front of her, as she tried to spot her sand dune. The figure of a man wearing red swim shorts was standing there, with his hands on his hips, looking out to sea.

"Is it cold?"

Helen guessed that was as close to an apology as she was ever likely to get. "No. It's wonderful. You should go in."

Helen lay on her T-shirt, dripping water everywhere. The hot sun on her wet body felt good. She read for a while. Then she turned over and closed her eyes as the sun browned her back.

David sat, his arms clasped around his knees, just looking straight ahead.

The two children were still making sand castles.

*

David's demeanour had not improved by dinner time. He said he was not up to a restaurant, so they came back to the motel room with a takeaway pizza and a six-pack of beer. Helen was beginning to feel the holiday was deteriorating to nothing more than one of his mega-moods, with her trying to keep a safe distance.

She had never had to endure one for so long before. Over the years that she had known him Helen had become an expert at side-stepping his tantrums until, like a whirlwind, he blew himself out.

"How about a romantic walk along the beach later?" she said, ever-hopeful. David just glared back at her with his mouth over-full of pizza, and without him saying anything, she guessed that was probably a 'no thanks'.

"Well, I'm going anyway." And she did.

David was asleep when she returned.

Helen found herself breathing a huge sigh of relief. Maybe they did not have a future together. She crept around, determined not to wake him, and finally slipped gently between the sheets.

Helen had trouble getting off to sleep. She kept harping back to his behaviour. She thought she had seen the last of that David.

But things would be better tomorrow, and with that positive thought, she eventually drifted off to sleep.

*

Helen woke up to the sound of CNN blaring out of the TV David was already dressed in shorts and T-shirt, and was sitting at the table eating a Danish pastry.

"Have you been out already, this morning?" Helen sounded incredulous thinking it was only about 7 a.m.

"Yes, I've been out. It's 11:30! I thought you were never going to wake up! Your coffee's getting cold."

Still feeling absolutely exhausted, Helen felt she better make the effort and get out of bed; at least he was talking to her!

She threw on a brown cotton blouse and a pair of shorts, and started drinking her coffee in between yawns. Slowly, she started to feel human again.

"I think we should drive out somewhere today and have a picnic.

I love picnics!" Helen did not want to give him the opportunity to say no, and began studying a map for inspiration.

"Oh yes! Perfect! Look at these names; East Dismal Swamp...
Alligator Lake... Pungo...I bet it'll be great!"

They called into the nearby store and bought some ham and
cheese, bread rolls, a couple of tomatoes and a twist-top litre bottle of
Californian Zinfandel wine. Looking out through the window of the
Stop & Shop at the heat haze rising off the tarmac, Helen rushed back
to the chilled cabinet and collected two bottles of mineral water, and a
diet coke. It must be ninety degrees already. David put down a six
pack of Miller beer onto the counter and a packet of mini doughnuts,
almost smiling at Helen as he did so.

She gasped, jokingly, and patted his ever-so-slightly rounded
stomach. Maybe a picnic was just what the doctor ordered.

Their journey took them back through New Bern then out on
Highway 17 North.

This was it. Swamp area. Mile after mile of, nothing!

It had sounded so interesting and different on the map. For as far
as the eye could see, nothing; no houses, no cars. The closest thing to
excitement was spotting a road sign saying 'Wolf Xing'

"What's a 'Wolf Xing'?" Helen knew, but tried to get David
talking. He always relished the opportunity to appear cleverer than
his brainy girlfriend.

"It means, wolves, crossing."

"Blimey!" Helen peered out of her window through the endless
square miles of grassland, as if a wolf was about to pop up at any
second.

At last, the atmosphere appeared slightly lighter. Inside the car at
least.

Outside, following days and days of summer high pressure, it was
beginning to threaten a storm. Thick, grey clouds were forming and
the humidity was unbearable. David played with the air conditioner
knobs.

Helen looked up at the darkening sky. "I think we should have
this picnic pretty soon, or else we'll be eating it in the car."

"Don't panic. It's *got* to change soon!"

Thirty minutes later, not a single car had passed, and they had
driven miles without so much as a kink in the road.

"Where IS everybody? It's a bloody cheek calling this a
'Highway'. Not like those four lane monsters out of Washington!"

The endless, straight, single-lane road was rolled out in front of them until it disappeared into the grey horizon. Either side of the raised, black tarmac strip there was a deep verge of thick, knee-high corn coloured grass. It was swaying in waves as the wind built up. The verges of grass sloped away down to a water-filled trench on both sides of the road.

"Which came first, do you think? The road, or the ditches?" Another chance for David to prove his superior intelligence. Helen was actually quite intrigued because it looked so odd; a massively long, raised road flanked for its entire length by uniform canals on either side.

"It could be they had to dig the trenches because we're in swamp country, and it stops the road from getting washed away." David was impressed by his own answer.

Helen was dumbfounded. Maybe he had a brain after all!

"David, this is silly. It's getting dark. We better stop!"

"There are some trees up ahead, let's just see what's there." Apart from the trees down at trench level, nothing else had changed. David pulled over onto the grass verge.

The leaden sky was turning from mauve to black. Shockwaves of wind were carrying drops of rain onto the windscreen.

David reached back and lifted the bottle of wine off the cluttered back seat. Helen opened the glove box and took out the two polystyrene cups, salvaged and rinsed out from this morning.

The wine was superb. Even out of polystyrene cups. They watched the drops get bigger and louder. Soon the torrent of rain was pounding on the roof, sheets of water rolled down the windscreen making it impossible to look out. The windows misted up. Lightning flashed all around them, and the deep, angry thunder made the whole car shake.

They were cocooned in a noisy, grey capsule.

"Ham or cheese?" Helen saw the funny side.

They made the best of it; paper wrappers and crumbs all over their laps, juice from the ripe tomatoes dribbling everywhere.

"God, it's so muggy! Where are those drinks?" David, having the same thought, parcelled up the debris on his lap, dropped the pile on the floor by his feet and clambered between the seats into the rear of the tiny car.

The return to the front was even more awkward, armed with cans of drink. He contorted himself back around the steering wheel and handed Helen a can of Diet Coke. He opened a can of Miller beer, and placed the brown paper bag containing five more on the floor between his legs.

He settled back into his seat and turned the radio on.

He wasn't going anywhere just yet.

Chapter Ten

Helen gently shook his arm. He had fallen asleep. "David, I think we should get back now. The rain's easing. David!" He opened his eyes wide and looked all around. Shuffling up in his seat, he rubbed his eyes awake, and over-exaggerated a yawn.

"Let me drive, you look knackered."

"Let *you* drive?.." He was awake now. "God! I want to get back alive, you know!" That was uncalled for, Helen's driving wasn't that bad, she didn't think, "Besides, you're not a named driver out here, and we all know 'Miss Goody Two Shoes' won't want to break the law. You stuck-up bitch!" He turned the key and the engine started.

"What the hell was that all about? What have I done now?"

David appeared to ignore her question, swung the car into a three point turn, and headed back along the dark, straight road.

Helen, now quite sick of loud rock music, turned the radio off. Perhaps a calm, quiet environment might ease the tension. "I think we better spend the day at the beach tomorrow." At least she knew she could always walk away. She looked at him for confirmation. It had fallen on deaf ears.

The night sky was pitch black. It was going to be a long drive.

Despite the effects of half a litre of Zinfandel and six cans of Miller Lite, David appeared to be driving quite well. At least he didn't have to deal with cars, bends or other hazards.

Helen began to think that something in her life had to change; she couldn't go on like this; forever on tenterhooks, terrified of saying the wrong thing, doing the wrong thing. He wasn't fun anymore. He liked beer better than anything, or anyone, else. She remembered the early days when he used to make her laugh. He used to be so cute. All the female students on their intake thought he was great. But SHE hit the jackpot. He asked HER out.

She looked at him now. The dim light from the dashboard panel gave his youthful face an orange tinge. He could use a haircut. And a shave. He was a handsome man.

Helen never wanted to see his face again. This time, it really was over.

She leaned back against the headrest.

She would tell him tomorrow, and they could make plans to go back to London as soon as possible.

"You weren't going to tell me, were you?"

Helen was drifting off to sleep. The words woke her up. "What? What are you talking about?"

"Your flat; you weren't going to tell me that you'd given up your flat, were you?"

"I didn't give up the flat. The flat gave me up! I took it on for a year, and the year was up last week. So what?"

"You might have told me. We could have done something."

"Look, David. You were the last person I wanted to see at the time. Or don't you remember how you treated me?" Helen had found courage to face up to him, he wasn't going to get away with murder, this time.

"Oh, that's right. Bring that up. I wondered when you'd get round to that!"

"*Me*? You brought it up!"

David slammed on the brakes. The rental car came to an abrupt halt. Helen grew concerned at the worsening situation. She decided to stay calm and be quiet.

David turned and looked at her as he spoke. "Okay, as we're on the subject, tell me this: why the fuck did you bother to tell me you were pregnant, if you knew you were going to get rid of it?"

Helen took a deep breath. This was dangerous ground. Before she could say anything, David answered for her, "Because you can't keep your big mouth shut, that's why. You've got to have a dig at me. Rub it in. Show me who's the boss, who always has the final word. You're all the same, you women: we're okay for a quick fuck, and then you don't want to know us."

"Wasn't I meant to say that?" Helen tried to change the tone with humour. It didn't work.

David was in full swing, "You wouldn't have got in touch, would you? All my phone messages, you *knew* I wanted to see you. That I was sorry."

"You're right. I wouldn't have got in touch. I didn't want to see you, and just because *you* may have had a change of heart about the baby, that's tough!"

Helen should have listened to her own advice, and stayed calm and quiet. David ever so slowly moved really close to Helen's left ear. In a low voice, his words were more frightening than had he shouted, "You bitch!"

Helen felt the tears well up in her eyes. To cry now would be to admit defeat. He wasn't going to get away with it.

"You are such a jerk," she forced herself to sound in command, "whenever things don't go your way, you have to resort to swearing and violence. You're so childish. I can't stand it! You are a spoilt brat!"

"How dare you!" David's hands had turned into solid fists in his lap.

"How dare I *what*?" Helen said mockingly. "You thick bastard."

A fist swung out of his lap, smashing her in the mouth. The shock of it numbed the pain. She touched her lip. It felt wet, and was swelling by the second.

"Get out!"

He couldn't mean that.

"Get the fuck out of this car. *Now!*" He pressed her seatbelt release.

She looked at him incredulously. "You're nuts. You know that? You are round the twist!"

"Get out of the goddamn car, bitch!" Her reluctance to oblige his request made him see red. He grabbed a handful of her long brown hair and pulled on her scalp with all his might. She screamed with the pain. Lashing out at him only made him pull harder. She gripped his hand, digging her nails in. He slapped her hands away. She hit out at his chest and face, he finally let go. She kept punching. He moved slowly through her flailing arms and clutched her throat with both hands. He started to squeeze. Her squirms and squeals only made him more determined.

She frantically felt down the door for the handle. She had to pull it open before all the strength was sapped from her body. She could feel the eyes of a mad man watch her try to wriggle free.

David still had both hands tight around her neck. Her fingers reached the door handle. She gave it a tug. It wasn't enough. With all the strength she had left, she yanked the handle again, and pushed her knee sideways. The door flew open.

David's grip eased. As he slowly let go, she slithered out of the car, limp and exhausted.

'I'll show her.' David sat still, contemplating his next move.

When Helen had regained enough strength to stand up, she slammed the door shut and started to walk along the dark, straight road. The headlights lit the way. What now? How could she get back in that car with an animal? What if he drove off? There hadn't been another car on the road for hours. Helen thought she would just keep walking until he came to his senses. Then they could travel back together, and call it a day, sensibly.

David wanted to give her the fright of her life.

That would teach her.

He watched as Helen walked away. He thought about turning the headlights off – that would freak her out – but then he had a better idea.

He waited and waited for her to almost disappear from view. She was just a speck in the distance. How could she see where she was going? Surely the beam from the headlights couldn't reach her any more. 'I bet she's scared. I'll give her something to be scared about!' David slammed the gear into drive and the little car let out an unhealthy whine as he pressed his right foot to the floor.

The car lurched forward. 'I'll show her...'

Helen heard the straining engine behind her. She looked back and saw the lights slowly get bigger as the speeding car began to catch her up.

'Oh, my God! He's going to kill me!'

Thinking fast, she ran into the long grass of the verge. 'He can't get me here...'

David, a broad smile on his face, thought how scared she must be. 'Stupid Cow. That should do it.' He put his foot on the brake.

Nothing happened.

One of his empty beer cans had rolled forward and wedged itself behind the brake pedal. As he stabbed his foot down, all he did was dent the can. The car was still racing. He saw her stumble and fall into the undergrowth. He had to stop the car. In a panic, he peered down at his feet. In the darkness, he saw nothing.

There was a jolt. He looked up through the windscreen. The car had mounted the verge. Long grass was slapping the paintwork disapprovingly. The car was still travelling at over fifty miles an hour. Helen was somewhere up ahead. But where? She had fallen into the long grass. It took all his drunken concentration to stop the car from riding off the verge completely, into the ditch below. He tried the brake again. Nothing.

David's eyes fell on a patch of flattened grass just ahead of him. Helen had to be lying there. He struggled to get the wayward car back on the road.

Too late, the car rode up over a fleshy mound. Then the back wheel. The Metro bounced about wildly, knocking David's head into the side window. He desperately fought with the steering wheel. At last the car swerved back onto the wet tarmac.

The violent movements of the car had thrown the dented beer can free. David kicked it to the side. He could stop now, if he wanted.

He pressed his foot on the gas pedal, and kept driving.

Chapter Eleven

David was searching his mind to recall the events that had just occurred. Mesmerised by the white marker lines on the edge of the road, each minute that passed was transporting him further away from reality. 'What have I done? What have I done?' His memory was blurred, his thought process dancing about wildly, whatever had actually happened had scared him; he knew enough to recall that it was not pleasant. His heart was racing as he tried desperately to sift through the dreadful flashes of memory.

He still had not passed another car, he really did not want to pass one now.

Up ahead, far in the distance, he could see a pulsating light. His first reaction was one of panic, but when he looked harder, the light became white, and was flashing in the pattern of a huge arrow.

As he got closer, David slowed down in case the arrow was highlighting a diversion, or, dare he think it, a road block?

The flashing arrow was pointing to Al's Bar and Grill. A shack of a building in the middle of nowhere. David turned off the road and came to a stop by the restaurant's door.

The whole place was deserted and in darkness. No cars. No people. No sounds.

The only light was from a neon Budweiser sign in the window.

With the engine still running, and the head lights on, he got out and walked round to the other side of the car. He was praying that he may have imagined riding over those bumps in the undergrowth...or that maybe it was just a log.

As his gaze fixed on the paintwork behind the front wheel, his nightmare came to life. He had not imagined it.

It certainly had not been a log.

Even in the weird colours of the neon lights, David knew that the dark splatters against the white paintwork were blood.

He wiped his fingers through the tell-tale marks and walked to the front of the car.

He held his hand out in the beam of the headlight.

The red smears on his hand were unmistakable.

*

The front wheels were partly submerged in a huge puddle of rain water.

Without hesitating, David began splashing water up against the car until all the blood was rinsed away.

He got in the car and turned back towards the road.

With a long hard look through his window, he stared into the darkness that hid Helen. And the truth.

He continued on his way.

Chapter Twelve

It was nearly 3:30 a.m. when David drove into the car park of The Sundowner Motel. There was a light on in the office, but he couldn't see anybody inside as the car crept by.

He came to a stop outside room 17, shut the car door as quietly as possible, and went into the room, Helen's rucksack over his shoulder.

In the darkness he remembered the route to the bathroom. He felt his way to the pull-cord for the light over the mirror. As if in hiding, he didn't want the room too brightly lit.

The face in the mirror was tired and drawn. He combed his fingers through his damp black hair. He felt the sweat on his back turn cold as the air-conditioning chilled him down.

He turned the tap on and waited for the water to run hot. Scrubbing his hands until they were raw, he then washed his face and neck with the now nearly scalding water. The pain didn't register. He had to get clean.

He staggered out and flopped onto the bed. In the borrowed light from the bathroom he could see Helen's clothes on a chair.

The ceiling was spinning round and round.

It was worse if he shut his eyes.

He tried to blank out all his thoughts, but the more he tried, the more he remembered. He cradled his head in his hands, and felt the bump above his left ear. He could feel the car ride up over Helen's body, then the back wheel. He pictured her mangled, crushed remains hidden in the long grass, her spilled blood attracting all the carrion eaters of the night.

He pictured her skull cracking like a peanut shell. Over, and over again.

"Oh my God!" His whisper sounded so loud, he cupped his hands over his mouth as if to shut himself up. He suddenly felt a dreadful urge to be sick, and leapt off the bed towards the bathroom. The fountain of vomit streamed through his fingers and fell like wet cement on the cold, tiled bathroom floor.

Chapter Thirteen

David lay on the bed for what seemed like a couple of minutes. It fact, it was over an hour. The morning light was already streaming through the gap in the heavy brown and orange curtains.

He was too frightened to let the daylight flood into the room, so he did what he had to do in semi-darkness.

He grabbed both nylon bags from the wardrobe and tossed them onto the bed. He put all his clothes into the blue bag, his personal belongings into his rucksack.

He hunted round the room gathering everything of Helen's. He put her passport, ticket, emptied purse, and toilet bag into her rucksack. He laid the small rucksack on the bottom of her red nylon bag and then covered it with all her clothes and shoes. When everything of hers was inside the big bag he closed the zip.

He made a half-hearted attempt to clean up the mess on the bathroom floor, then loaded the two big bags and his rucksack into the car.

He walked back into the cleared out room and opened the curtains. On his way out to the car he picked up both keys and, standing in the doorway, took one last look. Did he miss anything? Had she used any of the drawers? What about under the bed? The bathroom cabinet? He checked everything again. Except the wardrobe.

Finally David got behind the wheel and was about to drive off. 'SHIT! The jackets!'

With his heart pounding, he ran back and opened the motel door. He headed straight for the closed wardrobe. On two hangers, pushed right to one side, were their jackets. He grabbed them both. Helen's fell to the floor. His hand was visibly shaking as he picked up the familiar denim. He walked out to the car holding her jacket at arm's length, as if it were contaminated.

Sitting in the car he took some deep breaths. He wiped his wet brow, started the car, and drove towards the office to check out. He thought about just driving off, but that would draw unwelcome attention. He shouldn't do anything illegal and stupid. If only he had thought of that a few hours earlier!

Taking the motel keys and his wallet full of dollars, he nervously walked into the office. The old boy had fallen asleep in the back room, but jumped into life when David gently pressed the bell on the counter.

David remembered back to their check-in; no one had seen Helen, she stayed in the car. Once he discarded her belongings, Helen Slater would not have existed.

As he drove across the iron bridge leaving Atlantic Beach behind him, David O'Connor had just one thought in his head: 'I'm going to get away with this!'

Chapter Fourteen

David drove for hours. His head still aching, and the odd desire to throw up, made for a most unpleasant journey. The radio stayed off; he preferred his own silence.

By 10 a.m. he needed food. At last he felt strong enough to face it. He turned off the freeway at Emporia, just into Virginia, and picked out a MacDonald's from the endless choice of fast food restaurants lining the main approach road into town.

He parked the grubby white Metro in the corner parking slot, right next to a huge garbage skip. Casually, he glanced inside the enormous green container, and saw that it was half full of waste paper, kitchen scraps and general garbage. He pulled the sliding lid down and went inside to eat breakfast.

Feeling much better for some food and a strong black coffee, David knew he had to get on with his task. He walked towards the car keeping a close watch all around, for people, cars, and anything that may cause him a problem.

The car park was all quiet.

Still keeping a keen lookout, he took all Helen's things, and threw them into the green skip. The bag sat in the middle of the pile, conspicuous by its size and form. It was too far away for him to reach it, but he knew he couldn't leave it sitting on the top, waiting to be noticed by the next person coming to the skip. He couldn't afford to have suspicions aroused.

Panic was making him sweat, and he began to hunt around for inspiration. He found it behind the garbage container.

Neatly lined up, there were four small plastic drums, all full of used cooking oil. A long-handled broom was leaning against the green metal. He undid the lid of one of the drums and poured the slimy contents deep into the skip, drenching the offending items. A quick glance around to make sure no one was watching him, and he started prodding at the rubbish with the broom handle, lifting as much as he could on top of the bright red nylon kit-bag. Limp lettuce leaves, soiled tray liners, and crumpled burger wrappers stuck to the oil-soaked nylon like glue.

When it was totally unrecognisable, and completely obscured, he gently lowered the heavy metal lid and resumed his journey to Washington.

As he pulled into the car rental return bay at Dulles International Airport, he felt awful. Lack of sleep, a persistent headache, and the strain of the last few days had aged him by ten years. He was aware of his body odour as he handed the Alamo representative the car rental agreement. The worry that she may look closely at the offside wing, and detect a small dent or two, made him sweat profusely. The girl, distracted by the stench in the air, rushed through the paperwork, and handed him back his credit card. She exhaled loudly as he walked away towards the terminal building.

As his airline ticket was 'open', there was no return date printed on it, and the computer had no reservation for the return date.

"The flight is looking pretty full, Mr O'Connor, but I have just wait-listed you, and if you come back here in half an hour, I can tell you if you are on."

The British Airways girl was very helpful, but David was irritated that she could not put him out of his misery sooner. He had to get on that flight!

He spent the next twenty minutes pacing up and down the crowded walkways, and was back at the check-in desk in good time. "Good news, Mr O'Connor!"

He allowed himself the first smile in ages. He dumped his nylon bag on the scales, snatched his boarding card, and rushed towards the departure gate.

*

The 747 made a perfect landing into Heathrow.

David stood quietly by the baggage carousel. When he saw his blue nylon bag chug along the conveyor belt, he grabbed it and loaded it onto a waiting luggage cart.

Walking through the Green Channel (he had nothing to declare) he was convinced the eyes of every customs officer were trained on him. They were piercing a hole through his back.

His mouth went dry; he could feel the heat from his cheeks and hoped they weren't turning as red as they felt. His sweaty palms were sliding around the cart handle. His chest felt tight.

He couldn't bring himself to look at anyone.

Instead, he looked down. He was aware of every breath. Every stride.

The stride of a killer.

Part Three

Chapter Fifteen

The pain in Helen's head was the worst she could ever remember.

After her parents and twin brother had died, she started suffering migraines, but this was like no other pain she had ever encountered.

Her eyes were open – she was quite sure – but they were filled with blackness. As she tried to sit up her wet and aching body would not obey. She slumped back into the wet undergrowth as a distant growl of thunder brought back memories of a storm. One after another, flashes of David, and pain, and panic, flooded her mind. Pulling herself up onto one elbow, she held her other hand up in front of her face. There was the slightest of outlines, on this dark, moonless night.

It hurt her to swallow, and then she remembered David's grip around her neck.

The urge to cry made the pain in her throat worse.

As she drifted in and out of consciousness, the night ran its course.

When she finally came to life, she could make out the faint outline of distant trees. She tried to move her stiff and sore body. As she stood up her foot slipped into a ditch, and the smell of stagnant water made her feel ill.

Steadying herself, and picking her already drenched body out of the ditch, Helen could now make out a grassy bank. Terrified of unknown wildlife that may be lurking in the darkness, she scrambled up the bank, hoping to get away from all that was evil.

After an almighty effort, she reached the ridge, and collapsed on all fours until her strength was renewed.

The sky was beginning to colour up. Dawn could not be far off.

She could see the long, straight road. To the left of her, to the right of her, the road had no start, and no end. Like her nightmare, it appeared endless.

Facing despair, Helen forced herself to try and stay calm. She told herself that a car would have to drive by sooner or later. At least she was still alive. She had so much to live for!

She waded through the sodden knee-high grass to reach the relative comfort of the tarmac road a few feet away. In the half-light of daybreak she fell over something in the undergrowth.

She looked down at what had caused her to trip. And screamed.

At her feet lay a rotting mound of pulp, gore and skin that had once been the body of a wolf.

It had been run over at least twice.

Chapter Sixteen

"Look, Sugar. I just gotta go. Your old man gets off soon, and with HIS temper, I'd really rather not hang around."

Debbie-Mae was kneeling on the water-bed, clinging onto Ted Jackson's chest as he fought with his socks.

"Oh, he won't be back for hours. You know how he usually calls into Al's for breakfast on his way home." Debbie-Mae let the skimpy satin dressing gown fall to her feet. She pushed her naked breasts against his bare back. He started to grow hard again.

Ted turned to face her, his urge rising as he savoured her rounded plump breasts. Knowing they were her greatest assets, she pressed her hard pink nipples into his chest. The hardness in his jeans brought a smile to both their faces.

Debbie-Mae grappled with his belt as he ran the palms of his hands over her nipples, and around the contours of her bosom.

As his jeans dropped to the floor, she fell backwards onto the bed, pulling him on top of her, kissing his mouth through his gasps of pleasure. The water rippled underneath them.

A familiar sensation, experienced three times a week – more, if Debbie-Mae's husband had to do extra night shifts at the gas station.

"Shit! Look at the time!" Ted was hopping around on one leg, trying to get into his jeans before Bob Eckhart got home.

Ted and Bob used to work together at the lumber yard; Ted was still there as a loader, but Bob left a while back saying there was a personality clash between him and the boss. He actually found his boss in bed with Debbie-Mae one lunchtime, and ended up putting the boss in Carteret General Hospital with a broken jaw, a broken nose, and severe bruising to the scrotum.

Although no charges were made against Bob, it was thought best by both of them if Bob got himself a new employer.

Debbie-Mae slipped on the pink satin gown and hurriedly made the bed look slept in, but not 'shagged in'. (She had had a lot of practice over the years.)

Ted grabbed the packet of Marlboro's from the side of the bed, while Debbie May rushed out to the bathroom with the overflowing ashtray, and a handful of soiled paper tissues.

He tucked the black tee-shirt into his jeans, put the packet of cigarettes into the breast pocket, and grabbed his car keys and wallet before kissing Debbie-Mae, and giving her left breast one last squeeze.

It was almost daylight outside; Ted promised himself he would not cut it this fine again.

The faded red Chevrolet pick-up truck backed off her driveway. Ted Jackson blew Debbie-Mae a kiss through his window, and drove off looking at his watch. In two hours he had to be at work.

He reached the stop sign at the end of her road. There was a cream-coloured car approaching the junction, but he had time to turn right in front of it.

The car reached the junction and turned into her road. It pulled up on her driveway.

Bob Eckhart got out.

Chapter Seventeen

Ted was thinking of ways to cut work early today. Bob seemed to be working every single night, and it was taking its toll on Ted. He desperately needed to catch up on his sleep. It was alright for Bob; he would go home and go to bed. Ted had to go home and then go to work. 'At least it hasn't affected my performance.' Ted was smiling to himself. 'In fact, seems to me, the more you get, the more you need, the *better* you get!' He knew he was well endowed; Debbie-Mae had always maintained his was the biggest penis she had ever seen. And she had seen a few.

He was speeding down the long, straight road by the side of East Dismal Swamp, hoping to get back to his place in time to snatch a quick hour in bed before leaving for the lumber yard. It was almost bright daylight now, and he felt even more tired when he realised he had gone all night without sleep. Yet again.

Way up ahead, he saw something move by the roadside. He had often passed deer on this road, or the odd wolf, but this did not look like either.

As he came closer he saw it was a young woman, walking barefoot, her shorts and brown cotton blouse filthy dirty.

There was not another car in sight. What on earth was she doing out here? He pulled up along side, and opened the passenger door.

When she saw the red pick-up truck stop by her Helen burst into tears.

"Hey, Sugar. What in God's name are you doing way out here?" Helen had trouble understanding his deep southern drawl.

All her emotions flooded out together, she had so much to say, but only garbled noises came out through her sobs.

"Look, Sugar. You better get yourself up here and I'll give you a ride somewhere. Where do you have to get to?"

Still struggling with his accent, Helen guessed he was telling her to climb up into the truck.

"I... I... I have to go to the Police." She finally managed to string a few words together.

"The police?" Ted was a little taken aback.

"There's no police station around here, Sugar. Not for miles!" Helen bowed her head and covered her eyes with her hand. She made no attempt to cry softly. Ted felt uneasy as her sobbing grew louder.

"I'll tell you what I'll do. How about you come to my house and make a call from there? I'm only a couple of miles up here and then you can call the cops."

It was a better prospect than standing on the road with no shoes, no money, and stinking to high heaven, for God knows how long. She nodded without opening her eyes.

Ted put the gear lever into drive as he studied the distraught, helpless girl sitting next to him.

He noticed that her low-cut blouse was ripped, exposing much of her mud-smeared left breast.

He drove off, hoping she would not open her eyes and see that he had an erection.

Chapter Eighteen

Helen slowly started to feel relaxed. At last, good things seemed to be happening. She would call the police, they would arrest David, she would get all her belongings back, and in a day or two, she would be home in London. 'I wonder if I could get my old bed-sit back?' Her mind was racing ahead.

She looked down at her filthy, torn clothing, and rearranged her ripped blouse.

"Not long now, Sugar." Ted Jackson had just turned off the long, straight road into a side road that went over the trench. Helen looked at the stagnant canal and a chilling memory of lying in the stinking muck made her want to be sick.

"Oh, just one thing," Ted Jackson felt he should tell the girl the bad news *before* they got to his house, "my phone has been playing up. They promised they'd send someone out to fix it right away, but I'm still waiting."

Helen slowly turned towards him with a look of despair on her grubby face.

"Now, don't you worry your pretty little head, Sugar, things ain't that bad. You see, it works sometimes, no problem. I have to play with the wires, then it's okay Hell, it *might* just work straight off!"

Helen understood enough of what he said and just felt numb.

The ancient Chevrolet turned onto a narrow concrete driveway, by the side of a weatherboarded, single storey house. The front yard was just grass, there were pine trees to the rear, and a handful of similarly run-down properties lined the quiet street.

Helen climbed down from the pick-up truck's cab, and followed Ted Jackson to the front door. He opened the screen door, then let himself in with a key. Helen followed, remembering how stiff and sore she felt.

The front door opened into a small, cluttered lounge. There was an open-plan kitchen off to the left. The tiny house was full of dark, heavy furniture. An old sturdy wooden table and four chairs were in a corner of the lounge, and a vast sofa ran along one wall, with a small table in front of it. The coffee table was covered with old newspapers, a couple of 'American Playmate' magazines, an empty pizza box, and three empty Busch beer cans. It was obvious no woman lived here.

Ted walked over to a heavy, solid wood dresser which stood against the far wall. The telephone sat on top of it. He picked up the receiver and held it to his ear for a few seconds. "...Nope! It's dead."

Helen wanted to cry, but checked herself. She sat down on one of the dining chairs unable to think what her next move should be.

Ted Jackson did her thinking for her.

"Look, Sugar. Why don't you go take a nice hot bath while I play with the phone wires? I can always get it to work. It just might take a while, that's all."

"What about one of your neighbours?" Helen thought she had solved the problem.

Ted Jackson bowed his head almost apologetically. After a few seconds' pause, he spoke in a low voice, "Sugar, I don't think that's such a good idea. This isn't what you'd call a 'nice neighbourhood'. Hell, I wouldn't go to these houses. The guy this side, he's a drug addict. Next to him, I *know* he's served time. And they're the ones I know about. If you told them you had to call the cops I don't think you'd make it out of there in one piece. Ya know what I'm saying'?" Judging by her dejected look, she knew what he was saying.

Helen leaned on the table and buried her aching head in her hands, as if to blank out the world. When she opened her eyes, Ted Jackson was standing by her side holding a thick, folded towel. It was no contest; she decided to take him up on his offer of a hot bath while he got his telephone line working.

He pointed to the first door off the lounge. Helen took the towel into the bathroom and shut the door. There was no key in the lock, and no other way of locking it. She walked straight out to ask for the key. She heard noises from the kitchen. Ted Jackson was standing with his back to her, the freezer door was wide open, and he was putting a brown ice cream tub back on the top shelf, moving other

70

frozen items in its path. When he caught sight of Helen out of the corner of his eye, he jumped, and slammed the freezer door shut. "SHIT! Don't DO that!"

"I'm sorry. Excuse me but... how do you lock the bathroom door?" Helen was embarrassed that she had disturbed him. Strange, he didn't strike her as being a secret ice cream eater.

Making light of it, Ted Jackson walked into the bathroom ahead of Helen. He picked up a very full plastic laundry basket from the corner. "Here ya go. Jam this up against the door."

"Oh, okay, thanks." Not quite what she expected, but at least he knew she was about to take a bath. He smiled shyly as Helen brushed past him in the doorway. She pushed the stinking basket right up against the closed door.

Plumes of steam soon filled the small room; through the mist, Helen looked at herself in the mirror: The purple rings around her neck didn't look as bad as she thought they should, but her top lip was cut and swollen. She thought how ugly she looked; her hair a mess, streaks of dirt down her cheeks. She took off her torn, brown blouse and muddy shorts and draped her clothes over the edge of the basin.

She gently climbed into the bathtub, sank back, and closed her eyes.

Everything was going to be alright.

*

Ted Jackson walked over to the telephone. He struggled to pull the huge, solid dresser away from the wall. He could only manage to move it a few inches.

Able to get his arm through the gap between the dresser and the wall he knelt down and stretched far behind the huge piece of furniture until he reached the telephone socket. He gently pulled out the little grey plug.

Using all his strength, he pushed the dresser back, tight against the wall.

The phone really wouldn't work now.

*

Chapter Nineteen

Helen felt her aches and pains melt away into the wonderful, hot water. The bathroom was shrouded in a sweet smelling fog; the scent of shampoo and bath gel had banished the overpowering stench of stagnant water and rotting vegetation.

She lay back while the shampoo soaked in. She thought how lucky she was to have survived her ordeal, 'Thank God he drove by when he did!'

The steam and hot water drew the last of the strength from her weary body. Closing her heavy eyes, she slid down into the comforting water until it covered her ears.

She savoured the feeling of being on another planet; no earthly sights or sounds. Lost in a tranquil haven.

The urge to fall asleep was immense. She brought herself down to earth with thoughts of calling the police, and sorting out the mess that was her life.

Reluctantly, she tugged the plug chain out with her foot and the bath water began to gurgle away.

She climbed out of the chipped, brown-stained bath feeling invigorated. It was time to face the world. The soft towelling pile felt so good against her skin.

Chapter Twenty

Helen rubbed the towel over her long, wet hair.

The noise of the laundry basket crashing over made her look up with a start.

Through the heavy fog of steam she saw a man standing in the doorway. Wearing only a black T-shirt and socks, he was holding his swollen crotch in both hands. He kicked the fallen basket out of his way and walked slowly towards a terrified Helen.

"Oh God! Oh Please, NO!" She backed up, covering herself with the damp towel. She could hardly breath. How could this happen to her? After all she had been through. 'Don't let this happen, oh God don't let this happen!'

"Just relax, Sugar. This will calm you down." She wouldn't mind. It was only sex, after all. All the other women he had enjoyed it. 'Hell, I'm the best screw in town!' He lifted his T-shirt up proudly, as if showing off the prize. His enormous red penis was straining upright. It looked too big for his body. It was certainly too big for hers.

Her back was against the wall. There was no way out. He cupped her head in his hands and pushed her mouth onto his. His breath smelled of cigarettes, the bristles of his ginger moustache poked into her cut lip, making it bleed even more. He wrenched the towel away from her grip. She was left exposed and vulnerable. He pressed her against the wet, tiled wall.

"Come on, Sugar. You know you want it." He kicked her legs apart, his tall solid frame was up against her. She was no match for his determined strength.

Pinning both her arms against the wall he began thrusting inside her. Helen wanted to yell out; no sound came. The more she tried to extricate her abused body, the more painful the ordeal became.

Ted Jackson was gritting his teeth with every thrust, steadying himself against the slippery wall. He was too strong for her feeble efforts of escape, and too big for her unprepared, sore body. She felt the rush of air from within her rib cage as he grabbed at her breasts, pummelling and squeezing them with his rough, callused hands. He pinched her nipples so hard she wanted to cry out with the pain. Still his pounding body was up against her, solid and tense.

He ran his hands all over her body. Helen felt sick. He grabbed her buttocks, squeezing her flesh in rhythm with his thrusts. "That's it, Baby. Move that ass! Make me come."

Helen tried to blank out his face; she felt his offensive breath on her neck. His wet tongue began licking her ear, all she could hear was his heavy, deliberate panting. She closed her eyes tight, and hoped she would die. Soon. *Please God, soon.*

With one last almighty thrust, his thighs trembled against hers. His contorted face eased back as the tension left his body. He slumped against her, catching his breath. She wept silently, frightened to open her eyes.

He lifted her shivering frame off him and she slid down the wall, unable to move. She lay on the wooden floor, her body curled up like a foetus, too numb to cry.

Ted Jackson turned towards the door. He bent down and lifted up the fallen basket, picking up all the dirty clothes that had fallen out. He put it back in the corner, left the bathroom without giving the girl a second look, and shut the door behind him. She needed her privacy, after all.

Chapter Twenty-One

The entire ordeal had lasted no more than three minutes. The memory of it would haunt Helen for the rest of her life.

Unable to stand, she covered her trembling body with the towel, and just lay on the bathroom floor, sobbing hysterically, rocking back and forth like a baby. Where had she gone wrong? Her life had been so structured and sensible, and now, she found herself stripped of her dignity, mentally scarred forever, and alone and scared.

Ted Jackson was not able to get the hour's sleep he had hoped for, so he just would have to go to work, tired. He had coped before.

He knew that Helen would feel better by the time his shift was over, he might even have found himself a live-in girlfriend!

She heard him whistling out in the lounge. Still too terrified to move, she followed the sounds into the kitchen. The front door was opened, and closed, followed by the muffled noise of the crashing screen door. Helen was holding her breath, trying to listen out through her involuntary sobs. She heard a distant car engine start up, and then it was gone.

It took all her strength and courage to stand up and regain control of her life; for the last two days, other people had dictated it for her.

Clutching the clammy damp towel around her, she nervously tiptoed out of the bathroom. She dreaded bumping into him. She was telling herself that she had heard him leave, but as her mind had taken on board so much recently, she really wouldn't have been surprised if it started to play cruel tricks. After creeping around the entire house, she was at least relieved to think that her mind was still functioning. She really was all alone.

Helen stood in the lounge, breathing deeply. She had a lot of thinking to do.

She rushed over to the telephone. 'Please God let it work!'

It was dead. She thought about the neighbours. Had that story been true as well? She cautiously peered through the window. There was no sign of life. What should she do? Two life shattering ordeals in twenty four hours were enough for anyone to have to cope with. She decided to go it alone, stay away from the neighbours. 'He thinks *they're* bad news as neighbours. I wonder if they know they're living next door to a rapist.'

She couldn't bear the thought of remaining contaminated with his crime for another second. Her skin smelled of stale cigarettes. She blinked hard to erase the sight of his face right up against hers, breathing over her, licking her.. She ran back into the bathroom and showered him away. She had to get the hell away from there so desperately, but the need to rid herself of his smell, his touch, and his bodily fluids was even greater. It had to be done.

She hurriedly dried herself, and then put her muddy shorts and blouse back on, but then caught sight of herself in the mirror. The rips and tears in her brown blouse appeared worse than she had realised. She had to think of something.

Still terrified that he might walk in at any moment, she crept in his bedroom. The smell of cigarettes was overpowering.

She opened all the cupboards, not really knowing what she was looking for – until she found it. In a drawer were several T-shirts, all the same style but in different colours. She lifted out the top two, noticed the second one was black, and replaced it for another white one. She put one on and went into the kitchen.

Thinking quite clearly now, driven on by the consuming desire to survive, she set about her task.

Not knowing what the next few days would bring, she at least knew that she needed food and drink. She went to the fridge/freezer and opened the fridge door. She suddenly remembered the rapist at the freezer door. Something about that didn't make sense to her. Intrigued, she slowly opened the freezer door and reached deep inside. Pulling out the familiar brown ice cream tub, she lifted off the lid. On a good day she would have been delighted to find it full of 'Coffee Toffee Crunch'. But it hadn't been a good day.

There was no ice cream at all. Just money. $87 exactly.

'No wonder he was so jumpy when I disturbed him.'

Amazed at her find, she quickly stuffed the notes into her pocket, and then put the empty Ben & Jerry's tub back in the freezer. She continued her hunt for food.

There was soon a big pile on the kitchen table: a packet of Ruffles potato chips, two bottles of coke, a packet of Chips Ahoy cookies, and three tomatoes. Everything else in the fridge looked like a laboratory culture.

In the cupboard under the sink she found an old shoulder bag.

She shook the contents out over the floor: a half empty tin of bait, two empty Marlboro's packets, a roll of fishing twine and a well thumbed copy of 'Playmates Weekly' fell out.

After brushing out the last pieces of fluff and ash she washed her hands and then filled the grubby bag with the food, drink and T-shirt. Thinking all the time, she breathed deeply, then went back into his bedroom, still looking for anything that may help her on her journey. His shoes were way too big. There was nothing else, then, just as she was about to walk out her gaze fixed upon a piece of paper on his bed-side table.

She cautiously picked up the hand written letter. It was scented, pink paper, with dreadful handwriting. The matching envelope was underneath. The sender's address was on the back.

It was addressed to: Ted Jackson, 147 River Road, Tyrrell Heights, 28461.

It began, "My Darling Ted',

Helen skipped through the love letter feeling repulsed by the graphic references to obscene sex acts.

It was signed, 'Your fluffy bunny, Debbie-Mae' and followed by several X's.

Helen folded the letter and envelope. Not quite sure what help it might be, she put it in the bag anyway.

Taking one last look around the miserable shack, she walked out of the front door, making as little noise as possible. With the old fishing bag on her shoulder, no shoes on her feet, and wearing Ted Jackson's T-shirt, she kept her head down, and tentatively began the long walk back to the highway.

Once clear of the handful of houses, Helen thought about how her life had changed.

Barefoot and alone, she was marooned in a foreign country, with only a stolen $87 keeping her from total destitution.

Raped, having already been left for dead, how could she ever again give her trust or love to a man?

Chapter Twenty-Two

It was late afternoon when the family in the Buick Century brought Helen to Morehead City. Helen had already been picked up by two women who drove her to the start of Highway 17 south, but as they were travelling north, Helen had to go through the ordeal of finding another ride to get back to Atlantic Beach. Not sure what she would do – or who she might meet – once she got there, at least it was sort of familiar territory, in this strange, hostile land. Helen had smiled ironically to herself when she recalled the two women lecturing her on the dangers of hitch-hiking alone on quiet roads. If only they knew just how wise their words of wisdom were. Why weren't they on that road a few hours earlier?

The young daughter in the back next to Helen had stared at her constantly. Her fixed, disapproving gaze gave Helen the creeps. Even staring back had no effect, other than to make the girl's lips weld tighter together. They had never picked up a hitch-hiker before; Mommy said they were bad, no-good people, so why had they picked up this dirty woman with no shoes on?

"Because, dear, this young lady needs our help, and as The Lord's followers it is our duty to help her." The father gave the explanation as much for his wife's benefit as his eight year old daughter's.

The Buick drove through familiar streets in Morehead City. Helen remembered her excitement the first time round. Her dolphin. And David. She had to take a deep breath, and swallow hard.

"Is it far once we get into Atlantic Beach?" The woman sounded irritated, and short-tempered. Annoyed that her husband had been so happy to accommodate this attractive, young, female stranger, "...because we should have been in Beaufort an hour ago, a family reunion, you understand."

Before Helen could answer, the husband jumped in, "For God's sake, woman. One hour less with your mother can only be a good thing!" He noticeably eased back on the gas.

Sensing a full-blown argument, Helen leaned forward, the eyes of the girl following every muscle movement, "Er, . I think it is only a mile or so down here; just after the bridge."

The car turned into Fort Macon Road, Helen was still leaning forward, trying to spot the familiar building in good time.

"There it is. You can turn into Kingston Road."

The man indicated left, and pulled up along side the drab, grey building.

"Would you like me to come in with you?" he was already unfastening his seat belt.

"I think she can manage on her own!" His wife put her hand on his chest as if to say, 'Don't you DARE'.

"I'll be fine. Really. Thank you very much." Helen smiled and got out of the car. The little girl stared at her until she disappeared behind the door of the Atlantic Beach Police Station.

*

Officer Koblonski was behind the desk. It was almost the end of his day shift and he was looking forward to the big game on the TV His mouth was parched and he was thinking about the first beer on his way home. He always called in on The Golden Egg, Chinese restaurant, and Charlie Tang, the owner, would be preparing for the evening trade; he would gladly give Koblonski a couple of beers 'on the house'. He had never had a break-in during his two years there, unlike neighbouring businesses, and put it down to good relations with the local police. The odd patrol car parked outside, or a police officer inside, certainly could not hurt, and for the cost of a few beers, and the occasional take-away meal, Charlie Tang considered it a good investment. His extra insurance.

"Now let's get this straight." Koblonski was irritated that she had come in now. Another half hour and Williams would have been sitting here, while Koblonski was up the road, enjoying a beer. From what he understood so far, he was going to be here for some time. "This guy tries to rape you, then he tries to kill you?" Koblonski was tapping the point of his pen on the empty sheet of paper in front of him.

Helen had started quite lucidly, but was now babbling as emotions welled up. Koblonski's obvious annoyance was not helping.

"NO!" Helen's frustration was making her shout. She ordered herself to stay calm.

"First David O'Connor left me by the roadside, after beating me up, then this other bastard took me to his house and raped me."

"Were they working together?"

"What? Of *course* they weren't working together!" Helen wondered what sort of idiot this was, sitting at the desk. Were all men really this stupid?

"Did you go to his house of your own free will?"

"Of course I did. I was in the middle of nowhere. I didn't think for one minute he was going to rape me!"

Koblonski sat back in his chair, sucking on his teeth.

"So, who is this David O'Connell?"

"*O'Connor*! He was my boyfriend. We both came over from England for a holiday."

"But he didn't rape you, right?"

"No, he didn't rape me, this guy did." Helen took the pink paper from the bag, and dropped it on the desk.

Koblonski wrote down Ted Jackson's name and address underneath David O'Connor's name. Before he could speak, Helen explained how she got hold of the pink letter, and as she spoke, she picked it up and placed it back in the canvas bag.

"So, how did you escape from the rapist?"

"Well, after he went to work... I... left." Her voice trailed away as she heard her own words, and realised how ridiculous they sounded. Koblonski was still sucking his teeth, and tapping his pen on the paper pad.

"So, where is this O'Connor?"

At last they were getting somewhere.

"We were staying just along the road, at The Sundowner Motel."

Koblonski reached for his peaked hat and walked into the back office to have a word with the operator at the telephone exchange. He tore the sheet of paper from the pad on his desk and walked out, assuming Helen was following him.

He was picturing the chilled bottle of Rolling Rock beer on the bar counter of The Golden Egg, as he put his hat on and walked out of the police station. They both got into the white patrol car parked outside.

"Let's go see this David guy."

Chapter Twenty-Three

The white police patrol car stopped outside the office of The Sundowner Motel. Helen led Koblonski through the open door.

Pushing past her, he reached the counter first, as if to regain his authority.

"I need to speak to a guy called O'Connor, who is staying here."

"Room seventeen," Helen butted in.

The old boy behind the counter flicked back through the big book, and then stopped, holding his finger to his mouth.

"You mean the guy with the funny accent, don't you? He checked out real early this morning. Gee, it was barely light! Son-of-a-bitch barfed all over the bathroom floor. Had to clean the god-damned mess up myself. I'm the only one here, ya know..."

"Er, yup. You think I can take a look?" Koblonski had better things to do than listen to the hard luck story of an old motel clerk.

He went inside room 17. Helen felt very strange as she followed. The room was bare, clean, and ready for the next guest. It was as if she and David had never been there.

"What's he done?" The old boy had run after them, this was the most exciting thing to happen to him in months.

"Er that's confidential." What Koblonski wanted to say was that he didn't *know* what O'Connor had done; it sounded like a lovers tiff. OKAY, he had smacked her about a bit, then took off. But had an offence really been committed? Besides, he was probably on a plane bound for London at this very moment.

Helen and the police officer walked back to the patrol car. Koblonski did *not* want her to get back in.

"Look, lady, Miss Slater, do you have any money on you?" Filled with guilt, Helen couldn't look at him. "Y... Yes, a little."

"Okay Have you got enough to spend a night here?"

With her cheeks starting to flush, Helen looked down and nodded.

"Okay   You stay here tonight, it's getting pretty late.   This O'Connor creep isn't here, so he can't hurt you, and as for the other guy, Jackson, I'll have someone go talk to him. Okay?"

He was willing her to say yes. It really was getting late. His thirst was making his voice crack, and the game on TV started in less than an hour. Besides, he didn't think he could do anything here. There was no case to answer. He was quite sure.

Helen felt all out of sorts. She wasn't happy with the way things were proceeding so far, but she was at a loss as to what else to suggest. The matter was in the hands of the police. What else could she do? David had disappeared, but at least they would track down the rapist. Reluctantly, she agreed to spend the night in the motel, but declined the old boy's suggestion of staying in room seventeen. Koblonski walked with her to the new room.

Studying all the notes on the piece of paper in his hand, he turned his attention, briefly, to Ted Jackson and tried to get the sequence of events clear in his mind.

"So, tell me. Did he rip your clothes when he attacked you, and how many items of clothing did Jackson remove before the rape?"

Knowing she wasn't going to enjoy her own answer, Helen almost whispered her response.

"I wasn't wearing any clothes. I had just got out of the bath."

After a long pause, while Koblonski reviewed all the information, he finally summed up:

"So, you got into this strange man's vehicle, of your own free will, you go to his house, of your own free will, *you* remove all your clothing, you say he raped you, and when he left for work, .. you just opened the door,... and walked away."

It had happened like that. But Helen knew it hadn't happened like that!

Without saying anything – what could she say – Helen sat at the table and looked out of her window at the reddening sky. She felt numb, exhausted, and totally drained.

Officer Koblonski opened the door to leave. He looked back at the young English girl. She kept staring through the motel window, and tears had once again filled her puffy, red eyes.

"I'll call round in the morning. You take it easy, okay? Get a good night's rest. You look as if you could use it. Don't worry. We'll sort this mess out."

As he walked away, he folded the piece of paper with all his notes on it, and put it in his top pocket. He knew she was looking in his direction, so he better not throw it away just yet. He knew there was a waste bin outside The Golden Egg.

Chapter Twenty-Four

Helen lay on the bed as the room grew dark. She did not bother to put the lights on. She could do her thinking in the dark. She went over in her mind the meeting with the police officer. It had not gone well. Even she was now having doubts about the events. It was clear to her that he had not believed her. About anything. 'He never told me to go to the hospital – not that they would have found much in the way of evidence – but he didn't even ask me to sign a report! Maybe I could see another policeman. What's the point? I've blown it!'

As her thoughts carried her through the night, time meant nothing any more. The early morning birdsong distracted her for a moment, and she saw it was getting light. Maybe she had slept during the night. But it did not feel like it.

A loud knock at the door startled her.

It was Officer Koblonski.

Surprised at seeing him again, Helen let him in and sat down in silence to hear what he had to say.

"I got an officer from Craven County Sheriff's Department to go see your Mr Jackson."

Helen looked up in amazement. She was about to speak when Koblonski put his hands up, to stop her in her tracks, and continued:

"He agreed he gave you a ride to his house, and he agreed he had sex with you."

Helen was itching to speak, but Koblonski's hand went up again. "He said you agreed to sex, after inviting him into the bathroom where you were standing, naked as a jay bird."

"Of *course* I was naked, I'd just..."

"He has filed charges against *you*."

Helen was speechless. She just stared at the police officer, while his last sentence sunk in.

"He has *what*?" She really did need to hear this again.

"He has filed charges against you" Koblonski, almost embarrassed for the girl, looked down at the notepad in his hand even though he knew full well what was on it:

"Larceny. Three counts."

Helen sat on the edge of the bed, staring blankly into space, gently shaking her head from side to side in disbelief.

Koblonski, still unable to look at the girl, lowered his voice as he went on:

"He claims you stole food, items of clothing, and money, $100."

"It was only eighty seven, you dick-head."

"What was that?"

"Nothing." Helen hadn't realised her thoughts had grown so loud.

The police officer sat down next to her.

"Look, Miss Slater. I don't know exactly what the hell is going on here, but you sure don't look like you deserve this kinda hassle. This Jackson sounds like a real asshole. He's well known to the guys at Craven County. But I can't do anything about this rape charge; you'd get laughed outta court. If it ever got there. There is no evidence to suggest he forced you to have sex with him. No evidence at all. Just your word against his. You admit all the marks on your body were caused by your boyfriend, you admit you went to his house and got undressed of your own free will. I'm sorry. The courts just wouldn't see it as rape. I'm really sorry."

Helen was silently crying into her hands. She had done a lot of that lately.

"What am I going to do?"

Koblonski could hear the despair in her quivering voice. He had to help her, somehow.

"You're British, right? Let me talk to your Embassy. They can fix you up with an emergency passport. What about money? Can you have your bank wire you out some funds?"

Helen smiled, ironically, "The only thing I own in a bank, is a huge overdraft. They have already said they won't let me have another penny until next year's grant is paid in, and that's weeks away."

"What about your folks? Can't they help?"

Helen was suddenly reminded of just how alone in the world she was. She shook her head.

Koblonski was desperately thinking of something that might cheer her up. He hadn't exactly been of much use, so far.

Helen stood up and shuffled to the window.

"What about the charges he's filed against me?"

"You let me sort that out. How do I know where you are? If I can't find you how can I arrest you?"

Helen looked at him, wanting to smile, but she just could not manage it.

Koblonski felt really bad; it crossed his mind that maybe had he shown a little more understanding last night he could have helped this girl. He did not enjoy his evening anyway. At least his guilt made him follow it up. And look where that got her! No rape charge – just three against *her*! He was feeling even worse when she began to cry again. Maybe it was all true! He had let her down; she had been alone in a foreign land, with terrible things happening to her and all he could think about was a free drink and a ball game!

"I don't know if this is gonna be of interest, and don't quote me on it, I don't want to make things worse, for either of us, but a friend of mine owns a restaurant on the beach a couple of blocks that way. His full-time waitress is about to give birth any day, and he needs a replacement real bad. If you like I can tell him about you, I'm sure he'll pay you cash, until you get fixed up with a passport. What do you think?"

Helen could not think. Koblonski went on:

"Chrissie, that's the girl that is having the baby, she rents a room under the restaurant, and I know she won't be needing it when the baby is born. I know Leon won't charge much for it."

Something triggered a spark in Helen's memory.

"Who?"

"Leon. Leon Jones. He owns the restaurant, Leon's Beach Hut Restaurant. Nice guy. I've known him and his wife, Rita, for years."

Helen remembered where she saw the name before: That was the place she and David had dinner on the beach. The pregnant waitress. Of course!

Helen knew she could not stay here forever, and her confidence at getting the Embassy to sort out all her problems was not strong. As illegal as it may be, she could at least get some money behind her, while she thought about her next move.

Somehow she had to get even with Ted Jackson. The legal way had failed her, she would have to think of something else. David O'Connor would be next. Wherever he was.

She was in deep thought for a long time. Finally, happy with her new plan of action, she spoke, with a confidence in her voice Koblonski had not heard before:

"Waiting on tables wasn't exactly what I had in mind for a career. But it would get me out of this hole, until I can get home. What about the room? How do you know she won't need it after the baby is born?"

Koblonski played with his hat, nervously, and looked down.

"Because, Chrissie's moving in with me. We're getting married."

Chapter Twenty-Five

Rita Jones was a tall, strikingly beautiful black woman.

Although in her early fifties, her hair and skin was that of a woman much younger. She spoke with a soft, gentle voice which rounded the harshness of the deep South. A hard worker all her life, she longed for the day when she and her husband of thirty years could relax and enjoy life at a slower, calmer pace.

She led the way into the tiny, dimly lit room, followed by Helen, who felt strange returning to the restaurant under these circumstances.

"Why don't you come up and join us for some tea when you've unpacked? I've got Mary to cover for tonight so you can start tomorrow. Come and see how it's done!"

"Thanks, Mrs. Jones, I really appreciate this!"

"No one I like calls me Mrs. Jones, so please call me 'Rita', and you're helping us out of a real hole, I can tell you!"

She had a last inspection of the room and bathroom, to make sure Chrissie had left it in a good state, and then she walked out, smiling at Helen as she closed the door behind her.

Helen looked at Ted Jackson's fishing bag, which she had tossed on to the bed. As she took out the T-shirts and food, the pink paper and envelope fell to the floor. She put the letter back in the envelope and placed it under her pillow. On her way to the restaurant, she had bought three T-shirts, some baggy shorts, and a pair of beach shoes, plus some toiletries to see her through. There was not much left of the stolen $87 but at least she had a roof over her head, and the promise of more money to come. With great satisfaction, she stuffed his T-shirts back in the grubby canvas bag, and dumped it in the garbage bin outside the kitchen, on her way to have tea with Rita Jones.

Mike, the short order cook, was busy in the kitchen and did not notice Helen go by.

There would be plenty of time for introductions later.

Rita Jones was sitting at a table at the back of the main restaurant, refilling the salt, pepper and tomato sauce dispensers. The restaurant did not open for another two hours. Lunch was over, but dinner had not yet begun. As Helen walked over to Rita she thought how orderly and clean everything looked, given that the restaurant had sounded full for lunch.

"Hi! Is your room okay?"

"Yes, thank you, it's lovely. Um, am I going to be alright in these clothes? They're all I have, for now."

"I don't know what kind of place you think this is, but you'll be just fine. People come here for a burger and a beer, nothing fancy. With your legs, they might even come back!"

They drank lemon tea, and Rita went over the ground rules; how to take orders, what was on the menu, how to cope with a customer suffering from too much sun and beer. She handed Helen an order pad and a couple of pencils, and a little white apron, with three pocket panels across the front.

"You don't have to wear it, but those pockets sure come in handy – especially for all those tips!"

Helen went to bed early. Tomorrow was going to be a tiring day. Lying in her bed she could hear people above her; the restaurant was quite full. She went over in her mind all her duties: Using the credit card machine, adding up the bills, getting the orders right, understanding what they say! She was thinking how much more difficult it all appeared than giving a diagnosis, and prognosis, for a patient. Her first ever injection had not filled her with the same apprehension as the prospect of opening the first bottle of wine in front of a diner.

From doctor to waitress in just over a week. As she cried herself to sleep, she wondered what her future held in store.

Chapter Twenty-Six

Helen was awakened by the noise outside her window: The clanging of beer crates and male voices sounded almost as if they were inside her room. She jumped out of bed, wearing one of her new T-shirts as a night dress, and lifted back the curtain over the tiny window. A grey-haired black man was chatting to the driver of the delivery truck. Helen guessed that must be Leon Jones. She watched the truck drive off, then the black man turned and walked towards the restaurant steps, pausing briefly to wipe the glass over the menu board with the cuff of his white shirt. He stood back admiring the clean glass.

It was another beautiful day: the sun was shining, and people were already walking along the beach. The early morning fishermen were packing up, and their car spaces were being filled by cars carrying families, here for the day.

Helen walked upstairs to the restaurant, a little nervous at meeting her employer for the first time. As she walked past the bar, someone suddenly stood up behind it, and made her jump. "Oh, my God!" she gasped, putting her hand up to her chest.

Leon Jones, who was refilling the beer cabinets, was amused by her fright.

"Please, not so formal. Just call me Leon!"

Helen smiled with relief. They were going to get on just fine!

"I'm sorry I wasn't here yesterday, but I had some business to take care of. Is everything okay?"

"Everything is fine, thank you. It's very good of you and your wife to take me on without even meeting me."

"Well, we've known Gary Koblonski for years, and especially since he and Chrissie became an item. He is a mighty fine judge of character, and if he says you're okay, then that's all we need!"

Helen was going to work the lunchtime shift today, so while she had a couple of hours to herself, she went for a long walk along the beach. Totally alone in her thoughts, she would focus on what she must do. What she would *like* to do. She could picture both David O'Connor and Ted Jackson writhing about in agony. Her manufactured daydreams would be full of images of her standing over both men who would be pleading with her for mercy. And she would stand, steadfast.

The lunchtime shift passed smoothly. Helen surprised herself. Both Leon and Rita Jones were impressed by her performance. They wondered what a well-educated English girl like her was doing wanting to wait on tables. But they did not want to deter her by asking too many questions: There were major changes about to take place in their lives, and a hard working, stop-gap waitress was exactly what they needed right now.

Helen went for another walk on the beach before the dinner shift. She was eager to call up her daydream. This time she had O'Connor and Jackson bound and gagged. She was standing over them with a whip in her hand. She trod on an upturned shell. The pain interrupted her daydream. Looking back towards the restaurant, it was too far away to make out. She must have walked for over an hour. She looked down at her Swatch watch. The face was badly scratched but it still worked. It had been through a lot, lately. 'Just as well I had a watch that was "everything" resistant. I must get a new glass for it when I get back to England; then it will be as good as new. If only I was as easy to fix!'

Chapter Twenty-Seven

Helen was sitting on her bed, staring at the pink paper. She knew what it said, word for word, but she kept looking at it for inspiration. She knew both addresses off by heart, including the zip codes, but what she did not know was what she was going to do about Jackson and his disgusting girlfriend.

"Helen, there's someone to see you, upstairs." Rita Jones spoke through the door, breaking Helen's train of thought, abruptly.

"Thanks, I'll be right up." Helen put the pink letter and envelope back under her pillow before going up to the restaurant. It was another hot, sunny day. She could get used to this.

Gary Koblonski was sitting outside on the balcony, drinking a free cup of coffee. He was not in uniform, and Helen thought how normal he looked in shorts and polo shirt, and Reebok trainers.

Helen poured herself a cup of coffee and went out to join him. They sat at the same rustic table that she and David O'Connor had eaten dinner. That seemed like an eternity ago.

Koblonski had come round to give Helen an update on his dealings with the British Embassy in Washington. He felt things would progress more smoothly if a police officer spoke for her. He also felt somehow responsible for Helen. He told her that an application for a replacement passport was going through and should take a couple of weeks. He did not tell her that he failed to mention David O'Connor to the Embassy official: Bastard he may be, but how can you arrest someone for being a jerk? Koblonski hoped that once Helen had her new passport, she would forget the jerk, and get on with her life.

"Oh. One other thing." Officer Koblonski was about to leave to take Chrissie for hopefully, her last antenatal examination. "Can you drive a stick-shift?"

Not familiar with that make of car, Helen was puzzled by the question.

"What's a *'Stikshiff?'*"

"A car with a gear-lever, ya know? Not automatic transmission."

"Oh, you mean, a manual. Yes, I have only ever driven a manual car. Why?"

"Well, Chrissie's got this beat-up old car, she won't be needing it for a few weeks. I just thought it you needed to get away from this place, do some shopping, or whatever, you're welcome to borrow it."

Helen was quite touched by his generosity and kindness: Not the impression she first had of him.

"That's really sweet of you. Thanks! I must meet this Chrissie some time. I owe her a lot!"

"Listen. The car is a heap of junk. I'll be glad not to have it parked out the front of my house for a few weeks! When you're done with it, drive it back with a full tank of gas, and we'll call it quits."

He handed Helen a piece of paper with his home address and telephone number.

"I'll leave it out front tonight on my way to work, graveyard shift yuk!"

That evening, Helen was dealing with the last two tables when Mike, the cook, gave her a bunch of keys. "These are from Gary. He said not to get worried if you open the hood and find the engine missing."

"What?" Helen began to panic.

Mike, who fancied the English girl from afar, was enjoying the opportunity to talk to her, his shyness often causing him such grief.

"It's a Volkswagen Beetle – the engine's in the trunk!"

The last couple were on their fourth refill of coffee when Rita told Helen to go to bed; she would see them out and lock up. Leon was eating a late supper in the kitchen. Helen felt neither hungry nor tired.

She walked out to the restaurant parking lot. There was the Beetle. The police officer had not lied about it being a heap of junk; its lime green paintwork was dappled with rust. Almost every window played host to a suction-footed furry animal, and Helen's embarrassment increased when she saw the fake tiger-skin seat covers.

The moon was high in the sky. The balmy breeze felt good against her skin.

It was another wonderful summer's night in paradise.

Helen drove out of the car park cautiously, getting used to the controls. It had been a while since she last drove a car. The Beetle, although noisy, went well. Helen enjoyed her new found freedom. Her mind grew full of possibilities.

Atlantic Beach was quiet, this time of night. She would have to get to know all the local streets. One thing, however, she already knew: revenge was just around the corner.

Chapter Twenty-Eight

Helen set off for her usual early morning walk along the beach, looking forward to more punishing torture for O'Connor and Jackson. Walking barefoot in the surf, no one could have guessed what was going on in the mind of this attractive, young woman.

"Helen. Wait up!" A hand grabbed her arm. She swung round to see Mike from the kitchen, out of breath from running after her.

"I've seen you walk along here every day. Do you mind if I join you?"

It was the last thing Helen wanted.

"No. Not at all."

Mike had trouble keeping up with Helen's brisk stride. She started walking even faster, annoyed that her space – and daydreams – had been invaded.

Mike attempted to make small talk

"What do you think is going on with the Jones's?"

"What do you mean? They have been perfectly charming to me since I arrived."

"Oh, no. Nothing like that. It's just that, well, he's been preoccupied all week, and she's been super nice to everyone, and the place is always immaculate these days when before it would look like a bomb had gone off. She used to say it was part of its beachside charm; to look a little chaotic. But now, it's so clean! And they are forever on my back to keep the kitchen spotless. And I mean spotless!"

"Well, maybe they have just turned over a new leaf. I shouldn't worry about it." Helen was hoping that he would not worry her about it.

She turned back sooner than normal; Mike was grateful that she did not want to go any further away from the restaurant. Tossing burgers on the grill was the most exercise he took, his rounded midriff was testimony to that.

When they reached the steps of the restaurant, Mike hesitated, willing Helen to say something. He so wanted to ask her out, but could not find the courage.

"Well. See you later, Mike." She walked past the wooden steps into her room without giving him a second glance.

The sky had clouded over by the time Helen went upstairs to start her lunchtime shift. There were always fewer diners when the weather was bad. Helen looked at the empty restaurant. She would far rather work hard and get more money in tips than do next to nothing. The time flew by when she was rushed off her feet, and her pot of money from tips was looking very healthy already. At the rate she was going, it would not be long before she could afford a plane ticket home.

Feeling bad at virtually ignoring Mike on the walk, she went into the kitchen to have a coffee with him. It made his day.

They both heard the restaurant door open, so Helen walked out to earn her money.

"Could you just bring us a couple of beers, Helen? And maybe a menu too." Leon Jones had just sat down at a back table with another man, who was in his late thirties and wearing a suit. Helen smiled at them both, and felt her face become flushed. The younger man was the most attractive man she had ever laid eyes on; he was tall and slim, with dark brown hair combed off his face. His features were strong and distinguished, set off by a subtle tan. Helen went quite weak at the knees.

When Mike saw her walk back into the kitchen, he thought something had upset her. "Helen, are you alright?"

Totally distracted, Helen realised she had come into the kitchen by mistake. She walked straight out without answering him.

Nervously, she poured out two beers and took them over on a tray. He was more handsome close up. Flawless skin, and straight, white teeth that smiled up at her.

'Shit!' she thought, 'how can anyone be that good looking?'

The man opened his briefcase, and soon, there were papers spread all over the table. He and Leon Jones were in deep discussion. Helen just admired the view.

A family of four came in, followed by a young couple. As the sun came out, so the restaurant started to get busy. Every time Helen walked past with a tray of orders she sneaked a look at the man, who had taken his jacket off and draped it over the back of his chair. His pale blue shirt and silk tie looked expensive. But then, she thought, anything would look good on that body!

When Rita came up to offer a hand, Helen went into the kitchen to sit down for five minutes and drink a coke.

"Mike, I think I'm in love!"

Mike dropped a bag of frozen French fries and stared at Helen with his sweaty mouth hanging open.

She smiled as she saw him trying to work that one out.

"That guy out there with Leon. He has looks to die for! It's a shame I've given up men for life!" With that, she threw the empty can in the bin, and sauntered out.

Mike did not know which bit of what she had just said upset him the most.

*

Chapter Twenty-Nine

When the restaurant closed after lunch, Leon Jones and the man were still talking. Apart from saying, 'thank you' when Helen put his order of beer-battered prawns and hushpuppies in front of him, the man had ignored her. She decided she would try the famous Atlantic Beach hushpuppies with her supper; if the man chose them maybe they weren't that bad. Mike had always urged her to taste the little corn-based snacks, but the name put her off. She found herself thinking like a schoolgirl about this good looking stranger, and forced herself to stop it. There was no way she wanted to get involved with another man, now, or ever!

She walked past the two men at the table for the last time on her way to her room, downstairs.

"Bye, Helen. Enjoy your free time. See you tomorrow." Leon Jones knew Helen had the evening off, and as he spoke to her, the man in the expensive blue shirt never lifted his gaze from the papers in his hand. Helen smiled and left.

The man leaned back in his chair and watched her, through the glass doors, go down the steps. He was still looking in her direction long after she had disappeared from view.

*

Thinking that it was for the best that he had not paid her any attention Helen grabbed the car keys, some money from her secret hiding place in the bathroom cabinet, and the pink envelope from under her pillow. She locked her door and then drove off in the lime green jelly mould. As she stopped at traffic lights at the end of Fort Macon Road she took out the maps from the door pocket and shuffled them over the passenger seat until the one she needed was on top. She folded it back to show the right area.

The creases were still there from the night before.

It had turned into a glorious, hot summer evening by the time she drove down the familiar straight road. Memories of the previous week provoked a dreadful smell in her nose, or was it really coming into the car from the stagnant ditch?

The land marks were becoming more familiar to her with every journey. Especially in daylight. As she approached the run down weather-boarded shack, Helen unconsciously slouched down in her seat as her heart began to pound. There was no sign of the faded red pick-up truck. It all looked deserted.

She drove on for about a mile, then stopped the car while she studied the opened map.

When she reached her next destination she drove along the road slowly, then turned around and did it again, to make sure she had singled out the right house. It was a tiny brick built bungalow, set on a large plot of grass. The houses either side had done a lot with their grounds, but the one Helen was interested in looked positively bare, and boring. The long driveway, from the road to the bungalow, had a car on it, but it was not the vehicle she expected to see. It was a small, cream coloured American car, that looked very old, and in a worse state than the lime green Beetle. If that was possible, she thought.

Beginning to wonder what on earth she was doing here, Helen found a turn off up a dirt track which led to a tiny electricity sub-station. There were thick bushes either side of the track, and best of all, if she backed the beetle in, she had a near perfect view of the brick bungalow through a gap where two bushes came together. Still not sure of what all this was leading to, she sat. And waited. And watched.

As it grew dark, Helen started to feel a bit scared. The car doors were locked, and she kept the key in the ignition, in case she needed to make a quick get-away. She had not seen anybody in over an hour, and in all that time only two cars had driven past.

The radio was on very quietly; more for company than because she wanted to listen to music.

A shaft of light at the side of the tiny house made Helen peer intently. A side door had just been opened, and she watched as a man in some sort of uniform came out and got into the cream coloured car. He backed off the drive and headed away from where Helen was hiding. Without hesitating, she started the Beetle and followed from a safe distance. On these deserted roads it was easy to follow the lights from far back. She was worried that he may see the same headlights in his mirror, but that was a risk she had to take; he had no interest in her, and there was nothing to tie her with him. As she began justifying her own argument in her mind, the little car turned into a lit road, which was flanked by several houses, stores and businesses. There were a few cars on this street, so Helen had to pay more attention in case she lost sight of the cream coloured one. She had left such a big gap, a car turned out from a side road in front of her. So far, so good; she could still track the little car through the windows of the one in front. The cream-coloured car slowed down and turned into the forecourt of a gas station. 'Great,' thought Helen as she carried on at the junction. At the first opportunity, she swung the car round and headed back towards the brightly lit gas station, thinking that he must have filled his car up by now. As she drove slowly past, she could see the little car parked by the side of the building. The uniformed man from the bungalow had walked inside and was talking to the gas station attendant.

The attendant behind the counter was wearing the same blue uniform.

While Helen absorbed what she had just witnessed, she noticed that her Beetle had less than a half tank of fuel. She turned back. She felt the adrenaline coursing through her veins as she pulled up by the side of a pump. It was high time she had a closer look at this mystery man.

It had been a long time since Helen had filled a car with petrol. And NEVER in America. Her grandmother had let her drive her car after she had passed her test, but Helen had never owned a car, and had not even driven one since going to Med. school. She was pleasantly surprised at the ease with which she had taken to driving the Beetle, but putting petrol in it had her foxed.

While she read the instructions over again, the man from the bungalow walked towards her. Helen saw him and panicked.

"Do you need a hand, missy?" The strong accent was similar to Ted Jackson's. Helen realised he did not know her from Adam, and took in a deep breath.

"Oh, yes please. I haven't a clue what I'm doing."

"Say, where's that cute accent from? Not round here, that's for sure!" He undid the filler cap on the front wing, much to Helen's amazement; she had been looking all over the rear of the car for it.

"I'm from England." She was tempted to take him to task over exactly who had the accent around here, but thought better of it.

She went on: "I've borrowed the car from a friend, I suppose I better fill it up."

She followed him into the building. He spoke briefly to the other attendant who had put on his dark blue baseball cap and was leaving. "I'll be seeing you."

"So long." The other attendant walked out of the door.

Helen went up to the counter and took out a roll of dollars. She saw the man from the bungalow had a red and white embroidered badge on his blue uniform shirt which said, 'BOB'. He was a wiry man, about thirty years old, with corn yellow hair that was wisping up from under his blue cap.

As Helen watched him get her change from the till, she felt sorry for him. 'You poor sod,' she thought. 'Right now, as we stand here, Ted Jackson is probably screwing the arse off your wife!'

She went back to Atlantic Beach via the same route. This time when she drove past the brick built bungalow, there was a faded red Chevrolet pick-up truck parked on the drive.

Chapter Thirty

"It's a girl!"

Rita Jones was standing on the balcony shouting after Helen as she began her morning walk along the beach. "Gary has just phoned from the hospital. She was born a couple of hours ago."

It took a moment or two for Helen to work out what she was talking about. Then the penny dropped. She walked towards the balcony. "That's great. What have they called her?"

"Catherine Olivia. Isn't that sweet?"

"Catherine Olivia Koblonski. Mmmm." Helen's preoccupied mind was still engaged elsewhere, "Shame about her initials." As Rita puzzled over them Helen walked back towards the surf.

The usual torture fantasies starring O'Connor and Jackson didn't feature for long this morning. Helen had more important things to think about. How could she repay Jackson? Somehow she knew Bob, Debbie-Mae's husband, held the answer. But how? She thought back to last night. Bob had flirted with her outrageously. Were all men in this country disgusting? Or was it just all men? Her mind drifted to the good looking man in the restaurant. She forced herself to scrub out the image of his handsome face, and that warm smile. 'For God's sake, woman. Get a grip!' He was taking over her thoughts. She steered them back to Jackson and O'Connor and the work she must do to get even with them both.

'He's probably married anyway. Or else he is a disgusting bastard just like the rest of them! Or both!'

Her faithful Swatch showed her that it was time to go back. By the time she reached Leon's Beach Hut Restaurant a plan of action was taking shape in her mind.

Helen skipped up the steps to start the lunch shift. From the sounds she had heard from her room, she knew people were up there already. She pushed open the big glass doors with her shoulder while tying her apron. With disbelief, Helen stared at the first table; it was a different expensive shirt, but the body was definitely the same. She had devoted enough time to studying it the day before!

She rushed past the man, hoping he would not look up, and darted into the kitchen to take cover. Annoyed with herself for feeling this way, she forced herself to get back out there, and get on with it.

Fortunately, it was very busy, and Rita dealt with the main restaurant, leaving Helen to serve the four tables outside. Even Leon had to do his bit and take all the drinks orders.

In between times, though, he was back, sitting with the man.

By two-thirty the place was thinning out. Helen had a pocket full of tips and the time had flown by. Gasping for a drink, she quietly strolled into the kitchen. Perhaps this was a good time to try the hushpuppies as well. Mike was quiet, almost hostile, towards her. Helen could not understand why, but was grateful for the peace, nevertheless.

To her surprise, the beer-battered prawns, and hushpuppies were delicious. The man obviously had good taste! Helen was shaking out the last drops of Sprite from the bottle when a crashing noise from the restaurant made her jump. Both she and Mike knew that it was no ordinary noise, and ran out of the kitchen to see what was going on.

All the remaining customers were staring back towards a table by the main door. Some had stood up to take a closer look.

Helen and Mike pushed past a couple of people, and reached Leon, who was kneeling on the floor, bent over. Beyond Leon, Helen saw the expensive shirt.

Helen rushed along side Leon, and looked down at the man who was lying on his back, unconscious. Papers had fallen off the table and had landed on his unmoving chest. Leon began shouting at the man in near hysterical commands, as if they were enough to make him open his eyes. Everyone else was silent.

Helen tried to move Leon away. He began crying uncontrollably. Mike and Rita grabbed both his arms and steered him away, while Helen took up her position, kneeling by the man's head. With one hand she pressed her fingers against his neck, while the other loosened the silk tie. There was no pulse. Automatically, she pulled the tie away, and finding a gap in the shirt, she ripped it apart, buttons flying everywhere. His tanned, still, chest was exposed.

People in the restaurant were shuffling around, trying to get a better look. Helen screamed at them to get back. Once Rita had pulled Leon away to a safe distance, she told Helen that she was calling an ambulance. Helen tilted the man's head back. As she put her fingers in his mouth, to her horror, she felt nothing: His tongue had slipped backwards down his throat, totally blocking his airway. Without thinking about what she was doing, she pulled, pinched and pummelled at his tongue until the fleshy mass was once again in his mouth.

Instantly, she began blowing past his lips, and then pounding on his chest. Then blowing. She had performed CPR on plastic dummies several times before. Right back to school days when she did a Red Cross first aid course. She watched his chest rise as she blew, but once she stopped, nothing.

She kept on. Blowing. Pounding. Leon had regained his composure and, standing among the diners, he was willing Helen to get a sign of life. Anything.

In the distance a siren was heard over the silence in the restaurant. It got louder with every second.

By the time the paramedics rushed in through the doors, Helen was still doing the man's breathing for him. Still pumping his heart for him. While one of the green-suited paramedics prepared their equipment, the other took over from Helen. She backed away, and was helped to her feet by two male customers, who shared the opinion of everyone in the room that Helen had done what none of them would have been able to do.

Exhausted and drained, Helen looked on as a paramedic placed two rectangular white pads on the exposed, tanned chest. The man's body suddenly jerked up. And then was still. A second jolt.

"I've got a pulse."

The entire restaurant let out a sigh of relief.

The paramedics opened up a metal stretcher and lifted the man onto the red canvas. They covered him with a cellular blanket and fastened the two straps over his body. Leon Jones threw the loose papers into the man's briefcase, picked up his jacket from the back of the chair, and followed the men in green suits out to the ambulance.

"I'll phone you from the hospital," he shouted out to his wife as he climbed into the back of the white ambulance.

The people in the restaurant returned slowly to their tables, Rita took charge, and offered free coffees to everybody. Some stayed. Some left, quietly, in a daze. Helen went down to her room. It was beginning to dawn on her what had just happened. She put the key in the lock. Before the door was open, without warning, she threw up.

'Some doctor I would have made!'

Chapter Thirty-One

Rita told Helen to take the next lunchtime off, but Helen felt that keeping occupied was the best way to tackle her problems. She just had one small matter to attend to in the morning, then she would be fit and ready for her shift. Hopefully.

The lime green beetle pulled up in the parking lot of the small medical centre. It was once a white-painted private house, complete with verandah and back yard. Now it was home to four doctors, and a childcare nurse. Officer Koblonski had recommended Doctor Aston. That was good enough for Helen.

As she walked up onto the verandah it crossed her mind that there was still time to turn around and walk away. Did she really need to know? What possible good could it do if it was bad news? She was deep in thought staring at the handle on the screen door, when an elderly woman came up from behind and just peered round at her, as if to say, "Either go in or get the hell out of my way." She went in.

The severe, overweight, receptionist was sitting behind the sliding glass panels of the counter, totally ignoring the two women standing there. Finally, out of the goodness of her heart, she looked up. "Yes?" Helen was about to speak when the elderly lady elbowed her along. "I have to see Dr. Warren, it's very urgent."

"Oh, it's you, Mrs. Davis. Take a seat, you know where to go." As the little old lady waddled down the corridor, the receptionist was shaking her head, annoyingly, as she ticked her name off the list in front of her.

"Yes?" She was looking at Helen now.

"My name is Helen Slater. You should have some test results for me."

"What were the tests for?"

"Can't you just look under my name?"

The fat woman, her white uniform straining over every contour, sat back and stuck her tongue deep into her cheek, while she considered her next move. After a long pause, she reluctantly let it go. "What name was it?"

"Slater. Helen Slater."

She pulled a card index box within her reach, and began fingering through them. It took forever to come to the 'S's. Finally, she lifted one out. "Doctor Aston's patient?"

"Yes, that's right." The tongue once again went into the cheek while she read the card. Every last word.

"Your AIDS test, was negative."

Helen didn't care who heard. She breathed out loudly, and smiled at the old trout. "Thank you." She walked out to the car, her hands trembling. She had trouble opening the door, and when she sank into the driver's seat she put her head in her hands and cried with relief.

At least the long-term consequence of Ted Jackson's actions would not be physical. Just mental.

Helen was met by Mike on the steps of the restaurant. "Leon wants to talk to us upstairs about yesterday, and that guy."

Helen had temporarily forgotten about the previous day's excitement. She suddenly remembered her good looking stranger and wondered if he had pulled through.

Leon Jones was talking to Mary, the part-time waitress who had all but given in her notice, but was happy to fill in very occasionally, when it suited her. Rita was reading a magazine, and put it down when she saw the others walk in.

"Thanks for coming, this won't take long." They all sensed that Leon sounded nervous.

'Oh God. I hope it's not bad news.' Helen thought about the man.

"First, I'd like to thank Helen for her quick actions yesterday. That was some performance!" Everyone nodded in agreement, while Helen turned red. "Now, I guess you want to know about that man. First of all, he's doing fine. He had a minor heart attack, which turned real serious because he swallowed his tongue. Thanks to Helen's fantastic care, he has come out of it just great!"

Helen was probably the most relieved, "Thank God!"

Leon went on: "His name is Martin Tyler, and you all probably saw us talking business for the last couple of days. Well, he is an executive with Cajun Kitchen restaurant chain. They want to buy us out and turn this place into a C.K.'s. Before you ask, Mike, your job is safe, if you want it. You'll just have to get used to throwing chilli powder onto your prawns! As for me and Rita, they have offered us more money than we have seen all our lives. So, when Mr Tyler is back on his feet, and the lawyers have had their say, we are retiring to Goldsboro."

Everyone started to talk at once, in the end, it was Rita who won out. "This won't be happening for a while, we just wanted to set the record straight now – you've all been so wonderful."

After the meeting, Helen went down to her room. She had only known these people a matter of days, and yet she felt as if a family was being disrupted. She was all out of sorts. At least the man was alive.

Helen stayed behind after the lunchtime shift. She and Mike sat on the balcony eating their lunch.

"Are you going to stay and get a waitress job when it's a C.K.s?"

Helen didn't want to tell him too much about her plans. "I'm just taking every day as it comes, Mike, but no, probably not. What about you, are you worried about it?"

"Hell, no. I know Leon will see me right."

"You think a lot of him, don't you?" Helen was truly touched by Mike's loyalty to him.

"You bet ya! Do you wanna know how they got this restaurant in the first place?" Helen really did.

"He and Rita left her family in, I think, Goldsboro, when he was something like nineteen. In those days, they were just expected to work in either the cotton fields, or else tobacco, but they weren't having it. So they took off for here, got married, and the old guy who used to own this place gave Leon the job as dish washer, and Rita cleared the tables. Well, they worked like that for years. They lived in your room! Then one day, ooh, fifteen, twenty years later, the old guy died. That was it. Leon and Rita thought they would have to pack up and head back. The restaurant was closed, and they packed their bags, and were about to leave, when this fancy lawyer arrived, and said that the old guy had left the place to Leon in his will! Some people gave them a real hard time. They had a lot of trouble in the early days, with them being black, ya know, but they stuck it out, and, well, you know the rest!"

While Helen enjoyed the hot afternoon sun even Mike seemed to be pleasant company. She sat back mulling over the happy story of her employers, relieved in the knowledge that she didn't have AIDS and that very soon Ted Jackson would, hopefully, have justice meted out to him; Helen's kind of justice.

Chapter Thirty-Two

Helen was lying on her bed, nodding off. The one beer she allowed herself with lunch was more effective than a tranquilliser. She had called in to a discount clothes warehouse in Morehead City, and bought a few items, careful not to dip too deeply into her savings, but the excursion had left her feeling absolutely exhausted. It was easy to blame the beer. The fact that she often got to bed after three in the morning these days, didn't seem to figure in her explanation for her constant tiredness.

All of a sudden she was startled out of her dreams by a banging on her door. "Helen? Helen, are you in there?" Rita's usually soft-spoken voice was booming through the door.

Shakily, Helen staggered off the bed, rubbing her eyes. "Yes. Yes I'm here." She didn't really fancy opening the door to have Rita Jones see her in this sleepy state, so tried to sound as normal as possible, and hoped Rita would just say what she had to, and then leave. "Helen, there's a couple of deliveries for you upstairs. You have to sign for one."

"Okay I'll be right out." 'Shit!' she thought, as she splashed water on her sleepy eyes, and checked in the mirror for pillow crease marks on her face, 'this better be important!'.

As she hunted the room for her keys she began to wonder what it might be.

The mail man was outside, sitting in his truck, waiting for her. "Helen Louise Slater?"

Helen hated her middle name and cursed anyone for using it. "Yes!" she said abruptly.

"Can you sign here?" He walked towards her, holding out a clip board and pen.

She signed it, and was handed a small padded envelope. The mail van drove off and Helen opened the jiffy bag right there. It was her new passport. She looked inside at the photograph; memories of having it taken in the post office booth came flooding back. She was wearing one of the T-shirts taken from Jackson's house. She closed it and started walking back to her room. 'Wait at minute,' she thought, 'Rita said, a *couple* of deliveries.' She climbed the wooden steps. Rita came through the glass doors holding the most enormous bunch of flowers. They were beautifully wrapped, with flowers of all colours cascading out, at least two feet across. "These are for you!" Rita handed the bouquet to a puzzled, wide-awake Helen.

She left Helen standing on the top step, dumbfounded, and turned back towards the glass doors. As she was about to go through, she paused, and looked back at Helen.

"They're from Martin Tyler!"

Chapter Thirty-Three

"Helen, is everything okay? You seem to be very quiet tonight." Leon had been behind the bar all evening. Every time Helen went by, she looked a million miles away. Even when she asked him for a drinks order, she was somewhat robotic, rather than her usual, amiable self.

"Yes, I'm fine. Really."

Helen was actually deep in thought. If anything was going to happen to Ted Jackson, it would have to be tonight. She promised herself that if nothing was achieved tonight, she would accept defeat, and get on with her life. All evening, in between taking orders for chilli burgers and hushpuppies, she contemplated her actions, and then fantasised about the results. Then she would tell herself not to be stupid and to forget the whole thing. She had come out of it alright, after all. What if it all back-fired? What if she found herself on the wrong side of the law? Was he worth the risk?

By the time the last couple left their table, leaving behind a very healthy tip, Helen had decided revenge *was* worth the risk. Whatever the consequences, she had to hurt him!

"I've saved you some beer-battered prawns Helen." Mike intercepted her on her way out. Maybe now that the good looking man was as good as an invalid she would have room in her affections for him! He had been thinking of ways to approach her all evening. Surely the beer-battered prawns would do it!

"I'm sorry, Mike, I'm busy tonight."

"But, it's almost eleven o'clock! You can't go anywhere now!" He had often heard the noisy engine of the beetle start up late at night, and would have loved to find out where she went until all hours. Maybe she would tell him now. Maybe it was another man.

"Mike, I'll go *where* I like, *when* I like. I don't need you to watch over me!" Helen stormed out of the restaurant, angry that he had poked his nose into her very private business, and angry with herself for her reaction. Mike was a good sort, just not her sort! Why couldn't he just leave her alone?

Mike was still in the kitchen scraping down the grill when the familiar engine kicked into life. He parted two slats of the venetian blind and saw that Helen had changed into new, fancy clothes that he hadn't seen before. 'Fuck it!' he thought, 'it *is* another man!'

By the time Helen drove over the Bogue Sound bridge, she was less paranoid that she was being followed. By the time the stagnant smell seeped into the car, she was convinced that she was on her own.

Destination one: no sign of anyone home, no vehicle on drive.

Destination two: lights on, just the one vehicle; a faded red Chevrolet pick-up truck.

Destination three: Cream-coloured car parked at side of building, familiar figure behind counter.

Taking a deep breath, Helen turned the car into the brightly lit gas station forecourt and pulled up next to the pump nearest the counter window. 'This is it!'

She nervously got out, conscious that her new mini skirt was far too short. She felt like a tart. If her grandmother could see her now! She looked down at her figure-hugging sleeveless top and wondered whether she might have overdone it. Terrified that she may be mistaken for a hooker, especially at this time of night, she cowardly reached inside the car for the lightweight cotton jacket, and put it on. She was so nervous at acting totally out of character, she had failed to notice that the man behind the counter had been staring at her the whole time.

She took another deep breath, and walked inside.

"Say, it's the lady with the cute accent!"

"Hello. Do you think you could help me out again? I'm sure I'll get it wrong if I do it."

"No problem. You have to pay up front, this time of night."

Helen handed him a ten dollar bill. He adjusted his cap, and led her out to the beetle. While the car was being filled, Helen looked round nervously for any weirdo that might be lurking, while Bob Eckhart studied her from top to toe, and back again.

"It's pretty late for a lady to be out all alone. You okay?"

"I will be. I'm just a bit upset about something, that's all. I'll be alright after a cup of coffee. Do you sell coffee in there?"

"Sure. But not tonight: The machine is busted."

'Damn!' Helen thought. It was going to be over a coffee that she would somehow steer the conversation to Ted Jackson, and what he was doing at that moment to – low and behold – Bob Eckhart's wife.

"But, look, if you really need a coffee, I know an all-night place a couple of blocks away. They serve *great* coffee."

'I *bet* they do!' Helen thought, sarcastically, but it wasn't really the coffee she was after.

"If you like,.. I could take you there." Bob Eckhart spoke timidly, fearful of a swift rejection. Helen couldn't believe her luck!

"Are you sure, what about this place? Aren't you on duty?"
"Leave that to me. I have to call someone. He owes me a favour!"

Bob Eckhart was almost running to the phone behind the counter. Helen followed slowly, still wondering whether this was a wise move.

Her thoughts were almost deafening as she walked through the open door:

'Why don't I just tell him straight?: This bloke, Ted Jackson, is at your house, right now, where he is screwing your wife, Debbie-Mae. It's not important who I am, but if I were you, I should go home right now, and fill him in for me!

'Oh yes, I'm sure he would welcome the news! But how on earth would I explain how I knew his name? Her name? Where she lives? Where *he* works? That they were having an affair?

'God! He might *kill* me for being a pervert, spying on him and his wife.'

Helen knew her only chance was to go through with her plan of action. She had been working on it in her mind for days, nothing would go wrong. Would it?

"Hi. Chuck? Bob. Yeah, I know the time, but this is important. Listen I'm goin' to have to call in one of those favours you owe me, I need you to cover for me right now. Somethin's come up, if you see what I mean!... Ah, come on! I did it for you!.."

Helen was over by a magazine rack, Bob turned away and lowered his voice, cupping his hand around the mouthpiece of the phone, "Sure you remember: Three weeks ago? Blow-Job Brenda? You know, the week your wife was outta town? ...Let's see, how *is* Jenny? I must give her a call, some time!... Great. Thanks, Chuck. I knew I could count on you. See you in ten minutes!"

Chuck walked in looking like death; he had been on the beer all night, and he was not a happy man! He sneered at Helen, who was still thumbing through the magazines. He thought she was a hooker.

"Okay, your car, or mine?"

Helen was on new ground now, everything she said had to be guarded: "We better take both," she said emphatically, "I'll follow you."

The two cars drove into the car park of Denny's. There was a handful of people in the restaurant, all with a story to tell, and none with a home to go to at that moment. They sat in a smoking booth, much to Helen's disgust, and before they had ordered, Bob Eckhart had lit up.

"So, tell me..." he sat back, drawing in hard on his cigarette, "...you said you were upset about something. You wanna talk about it?"

The waitress put two mugs on the table. "Coffee?"

When she had walked away, Helen knew her moment had arrived. She began: "I've just broken up with my boyfriend. Bastard. I've thought for some time that he was being unfaithful, but I didn't have the proof."

Bob's long legs were stretched out under the table, and his knee was touching Helen's bare thigh. He made no attempt to move it.

Helen turned slightly and crossed her legs. She just wanted to get this over with. She went on, "Ted used to say that he was working some nights, but then he would come in from one shift, and go straight out on another! Funny, eh?"

"Well, you should never trust a man called Ted," he joked. "What was his last name? Does he come from around here?"

Without thinking, Helen was blurting out the information, "Jackson, Ted Jackson. He lives in Tyrrell Heights."

Straight away, Bob's face turned serious as a spark of recognition darted through his mind. "Ted JACKSON, you say? Hell, I knew a Ted Jackson. I used to work at the lumber yard with him!"

Helen froze. Had she said the right thing?

"Hell, I haven't seen Jacko in years! Fancy him goin' out with a cutey from England! So, he's playin' around, is he? Always did have an eye for the ladies!"

Helen had reached the point of no return. This was her chance.

"Playing around? I reckon they're doing it almost every night! The one night in ages he actually spends with me, you wouldn't believe it! He actually called out her name in his sleep: 'Oh, Debbie-Mae!... Debbie-May?.. Like Hell! Debbie- bloody-*did*! Often!"

There. It was done. She sat back on the bench, sipping her coffee as Bob conjured up images of his wife fondling his ex-workmate, Ted Jackson. The coincidences of the names were too great. It HAD to be them! He was staring into space, just by the side of Helen's head. How could this happen? She had *promised* him! Never again, she had said. And Ted? They used to go bowling together.

A picture of his wife and ex-friend filled his mind: They were naked, romping about on the water bed. His water bed. He hadn't even finished paying for it yet.

Bob slowly stubbed out his half-smoked cigarette in the foil ashtray. Both hands then turned to fists. His eyes narrowed into a frown. Still staring into mid-space, he stood up, as though in a trance.

"I gotta go." He sounded breathless, "I gotta go."

He walked out to his cream-coloured car without seeing anything.

He didn't give Helen a second thought.

He hadn't even asked her her name.

Chapter Thirty-Four

The cream coloured car coasted to a halt behind the Chevrolet pick-up. Bob Eckhart didn't shut his door in case it made a noise. There was no sign of any light from his house. He crept to the side door and silently let himself in. The illuminated clock on the microwave gave him enough light for him to find his way through the kitchen to the rest of his house. His bedroom door was closed. Remembering the path to the door knob, he gently turned it and eased the door open. He felt up the wall for the light switch. Suddenly, the three people in the room were bathed in a harsh, bright light.

The water-bed gurgled and rippled as the man and woman were frightened awake. Debbie-Mae let out a scream when she saw an intruder standing at the foot of the bed. She would have screamed louder had she realised it was her husband.

She sat up covering her ample bosom with the black satin sheets. Bob Eckhart was staring at Ted Jackson; the moustache was new, but it was Jacko from the lumber yard alright.

Ted Jackson made no attempt to cover his naked torso. "Look, Bob I can explain..."

"You can explain lying naked in my bed with my naked wife! This I gotta hear!"

Debbie-Mae swung her legs over the side of the bed and was reaching for a pink satin dressing gown on the floor.

"*Git* back into bed, woman. I'll tell you when you can git out!" Bob was fuming at them both. He never had been good with words. They were certainly failing him now.

"Bob, just calm down!"

"Don't you fuckin' tell *me* when to calm down!" He marched to Ted's side of the bed – *his* side of the bed – and towered over him. "*Git* your ass outta my bed!" He stood back, champing at the bit, like a boxer being held back by the referee during a count on his floored opponent. Ted Jackson calmly peeled back the black sheet and turned to get out of bed. Bob looked down at his enormous appendage. Before Jackson could stand up, Bob grabbed him by the ears and head-butted him with all his might. Debbie-Mae was crying out hysterically. Jackson fell back on to the rippling bed, blood pouring from his nose and dispersing through the ginger hairs of his moustache.

Bob was on top of him, punching his fists into Jackson's cheeks. The pain put Jackson into a daze, and he was unable to fight back. Debbie-Mae ran round and started pulling at her husband's shoulders but in his blind rage, he was oblivious to her efforts. Jackson finally put his arms up between his face and Bob's fists. Bob started punching his chest, winding Jackson, who started to make choking noises. He managed to turn himself onto his side. Bob kept up the relentless barrage of blows.

Debbie-Mae ran out of the bedroom, naked and screaming. Holding her head in terror, she couldn't think where to turn. From the hallway, she could hear the dull thuds of her husband's fists burying themselves into her lover's flesh. She could hear the groans of a beaten man, powerless to respond. And then it dawned on her what she must do.

The lime green beetle drove slowly past the familiar bungalow. Helen was not surprised to see two vehicles on the drive. 'Oh God. What have I done?'

It was then that she heard the sound of a gun shot.

Chapter Thirty-Five

Debbie-Mae was standing in the doorway, her arms outstretched, shaking violently. The deafening noise shocked her into releasing her grip. A .22 revolver fell from her hands and bounced off the wooden floorboards, coming to rest a few feet away.

Her whole body was trembling as she stared at the scene in front of her. Suddenly it was quiet, the only noise was made by water dripping on to the floor. Soon the puddle reached her bare feet.

The two men on the bed were motionless. Her husband's body was slumped over her naked lover. Slowly, she walked towards the bed, whimpering like an injured animal. The gush of water died down to a trickle.

Terrified at what she might yet see, Debbie-Mae slowly reached for her husband's arm, to turn him over onto his back. As she touched him, Bob Eckhart suddenly turned his head and was looking straight into the eyes of his cheating wife, "What the fuck have you gone and done?" His words were deliberate.

Debbie-Mae screamed with fright and jumped back.

Without removing his fixed gaze Bob Eckhart peeled himself off his ex-workmate and slowly got off the bed. He walked towards his sobbing wife, who was cowering in the corner, his clothes sodden with water. And blood.

Ted Jackson was lying on his back, moaning. His groin was bright red, with blood, and as the Eckharts returned to the side of the bed they looked on in horror as blood pumped out of a wound in Jackson's upper thigh. He was losing consciousness as they stared on, helplessly.

"Ahh, Jeez. Whatta we gonna do?" Debbie-Mae was pulling at her hair, pacing around the flooded room. Bob Eckhart finally seized control. He ripped one of the cases off a pillow, formed at huge ball with it, and knelt on the collapsed bed pressing the wad of satin hard into the fountain of blood.

"Call an ambulance! *Now!*" he yelled at his hysterical wife. "And git some clothes on!"

She grabbed her husband's white towelling robe from a hook on the bedroom door, and quickly shuffled out to the phone in the hall. Still whimpering she dialled 911 and was eventually able to impart enough information to the operator to make herself understood.

"Just stay calm, Mrs. Eckhart, your husband is doing fine. Tell him to maintain pressure to the wound until the paramedics arrive..." Debbie-Mae was no longer able to speak.

Outside, neighbours were cautiously gathering after being woken up by the gun shot. None of them was prepared to go up to the house. They just stood in groups, most in pyjamas and bathrobes, mumbling.

The few neighbours who hadn't heard the shot were woken up by a piercing siren, as an ambulance and police patrol car sped along their road towards the brick-built bungalow.

Several minutes later Ted Jackson was carried out to the ambulance, still naked under the blanket. Two men wheeled the stretcher, while a third ran alongside holding up two soft plastic pouches, one full of plasma, the other a saline solution. Tubes from the pouches disappeared into Jackson's arms.

The huge dressing applied to the wound was making the blanket bulge up. Three women busily gossiped as the stretcher passed them by.

By the time Bob and Debbie-Mae Eckhart were led out to the patrol car the audience of onlooking neighbours had grown to about thirty people.

Half an hour later the road was deserted. People had returned to their houses. The bungalow was in darkness. No one noticed the little green car parked between the bushes.

Chapter Thirty-Six

Helen lay in her bed, staring at the ceiling, unable to get out and face the world. The bustling noises of early morning deliveries didn't have to wake her up. She never went to sleep.

She wondered if Jackson was alive or dead.

Her life had become one long catalogue of nightmares. This last one upset her the most; she had orchestrated the whole thing. How could she live with herself; she, a woman pledged to saving lives, had worked so hard to secure the ruination of a fellow human being. It hadn't just stopped at one.

She wondered if Jackson was alive or dead. She imagined Bob Eckhart rotting in a police cell. On a murder charge? She thought about Debbie-Mae, doing only what thousands of married women do all the time.

She had tried to play God. God had paid her back.

Outside, it was turning into a beautiful, hot summer's day. Cars were driving onto the beach. Little children were excited at the prospect of spending the whole day playing in the sand and splashing in the sea. Picnics were being unloaded. Beach umbrellas were being erected. Young lovers were rubbing sun lotion all over each other. Helen wanted to die.

She turned on the clock-radio by her bedside. Perhaps the distraction would help. She closed her eyes, as the endless procession of adverts for products which meant nothing to her were trotted out. At last the music began. She decided to get out of bed after the eleven o'clock news.

Trudging into the bathroom, she felt like she had the flu. She had hoped sweet revenge would lift her spirits, and cancel out the evil. As she studied her reflection in the bathroom mirror her face told her that it hadn't worked!

Helen counted her money. She spurred herself on with the promise that after the lunchtime shift she could go into Morehead City and check out the travel agents. Maybe she already had enough for a one-way plane ticket to London.

There was no reason to remain any longer.

She remembered Martin Tyler. No. No reason at all.

"Good morning, Helen. No walk on the beach this morning?" Rita Jones sounded disgustingly cheerful.

"Not today." Helen picked up a tray and loaded it with all the salt, pepper and ketchup holders from all the tables. She prayed that Rita would stop talking to her if she looked very busy. When they were all topped up Helen replenished the sugar canisters. Rita picked up her accounts book, and box of till receipts, and went downstairs. Helen sighed with relief, and poured herself a cup of coffee from the jug behind the bar. She heard noises from the kitchen. If she couldn't bring herself to talk to Rita there was no way she could look Mike in the face. Not yet. Not after the way she spoke to him last night. She took her coffee onto the balcony and leant against the wooden rail. The sea was a wonderful turquoise colour, its gentle waves dancing along the sand. An endless line of fishing boats bobbed about on the horizon. Everywhere she looked people were calm, and happy, enjoying the sunshine, without a care in the world. She despised them all.

There was a steady flow of customers throughout her shift. Helen had only spoken to Mike when she shouted out the food orders through the hatch. Mike had said nothing.

Two-thirty, and Helen left with the last customers. She added today's tips to the rest of her money, and drove off in search of an airline ticket.

At three o'clock, Officer Koblonski arrived at Leon's Beach Hut Restaurant in a white police car. He was in uniform and on duty. He had come to see Helen.

"You've just missed her, Gary. I saw her take off about half an hour ago." Despite Helen's rebuke Mike still found himself intrigued by her, and followed her movements from afar.

"That's okay, I'll wait!"

Chapter Thirty-Seven

Helen drove into the car park of Leon's restaurant still trying to work out how long it might take her to save the last few dollars needed for the ticket. Assuming she didn't go mad with her expenditure, and if she maintained her current level of tips, she should be able to afford a bus ticket to Washington, then a one-way Washington – London, in a week or so. As she set herself the target of eight days she caught sight of a white police patrol car parked in her usual space. Her mouth suddenly went very dry, and she felt her chest heave against the seat belt as her breathing rose to panic level.

She parked the green beetle alongside the familiar white Plymouth, calmly locked the door, and walked towards her room, racking her brain the whole time: So much had happened during the last few days, what on earth was the police car doing here?

Helen had almost reached the door to her ground-floor room when the glass door at the top of the wooden steps opened. Officer Koblonski was looking down through the slats.

"Helen! I need to talk to you!" He rushed down the steps and was standing next to her before she had turned the key.

Totally lost for words and inspiration Helen could only manage a feeble, "Hello."

"Can we talk in your room, or would you rather take a walk?" She chose the walk.

"I had to take Chrissie and the baby to the hospital this morning. Chrissie had some kinda woman thing that needed checking out. God! You should see the baby; she's so cute. I guess 'cos she wasn't that small, she didn't come out all scrawny and red. Ya know?"

Helen hated baby talk at the best of times. She knew Koblonski had not just come round to give her an update on his family life. She knew exactly what brought him here.

"While I was at Carteret I thought I'd take a look at the overnight admissions register: Friday nights can be pretty busy. Ya know what? A name jumped right out of the page at me, Jackson ... Ted Jackson!"

Helen stopped walking and stared at the police officer.

"Ted Jackson?" She tried to sound surprised.

Koblonski smiled like a smug game show host who had all the answers in front of him, "Uh huh. The very same! He was admitted with a gun shot wound."

They began walking slowly along the crowded boardwalk, Helen became aware of a wobble in her step as her knees turned to jelly. Her guilt and fear at hearing the words out in the open were more intense than she could have imagined.

"I read the report at Craven County Sheriff's office, and the statements. You're gonna love it!"

'I don't think so!' thought Helen.

"Jackson used to work with this guy a couple of years ago. They were good buddies. Jackson then starts fooling around with this guy's old lady. It's been going on for months. Then this poor bastard, who works nights, comes home early last night to find Jackson in the sack with his wife! Understandably, he starts beating the shit out of Jackson, his wife thinks he's gonna kill him, and panics. She grabs a short barrel .22 Smith & Wesson out of the drawer in the hallway, and starts waving it about, yelling at these guys to quit fighting, trying to scare them with the gun, then, boom! The gun goes off!"

"*She* shot him?" Helen could not believe it.

"Yeah. Crazy broad! No offence to you, but some women!"

"Is Jackson dead?" Helen wasn't sure what answer she wanted to hear.

"Hell, no. The bullet went clean through the top of his thigh; you know, the fleshy bit right at the top." Then Koblonski smiled, "...On its way, it took a chunk out of his, 'you know what'. That poor bastard isn't gonna be able to 'make out' for months!"

"So it wasn't a serious injury, then?"

Koblonski winced. "Not serious? You kidding? Try telling that to a red blooded man! I guess he could have bled to death. He reckons his buddy saved his life."

"What's going to happen to his friends?" Helen was careful not to mention any names.

"Not a damn thing!"

"What?"

"Jackson said it was a stupid accident and he's not pressing charges. We can't force him. If he refuses to testify – which he does – there *is* no case. Now, had he *died*... that would be different; we could be talking second degree murder! But he's not gonna die. His only problem right now, is how to *pee!*"

"I suppose his, 'manhood' will never be back to normal, will it?" Helen knew exactly what answer she wanted to hear.

"Every time he gets it out, he's gonna remember last night! Who needs scar tissue down there? Nope. I think his days of being a stud are over. Which is no bad thing, in his case; I mean, how many guys get their cocks damn-near blown off by their lovers? With girlfriends like her, he don't need enemies!"

"So, nothing is going to happen to the woman?"

"Nope. He doesn't even want her charged with assault or wounding. *And* she even had a God-damn licence for the hand gun! Maybe Jackson thought he got off light; you should have seen his bashed up body! I reckon he'd have been dead meat if his buddy had seen it through. He didn't need no gun! I bet Jackson would just love to know what made him quit work early. Was that bad luck, or what?!"

Helen reached a wooden bench and sat down looking out to sea. She was smiling to herself. No one would hurt her again and get away with it. She breathed deeply. Successful revenge was a most satisfying feeling. Koblonski sat down next to her, leant forward, twirling his hat between his fingers. They were both relaxed and calm.

Finally, it was Helen who spoke, "It sounds like I got my retribution for what that bastard did to me!"

Koblonski paused before answering.

"Yeah...but... nah. Forget it!"

"What?" He knew she would say that.

"Nah. It's nothing. I was just thinking... it would have been great if *you* could have had something to do with it, and then let the scumbag *know* you had something to do with it! Now, *that* would have been retribution!"

Helen smiled cautiously. "Honestly, Gary. What a thing to say! And you call yourself a police officer?"

"Sure.   But I'm also human!" He stood up, put his hat on, and looked deep into Helen's eyes.   "...Just like you!"

They held their stare for several seconds before Koblonski allowed himself the slightest of smiles.

Chapter Thirty-Eight

"Hiya, Mike!" Helen breezed into the kitchen, humming.

A massive weight had been removed from her shoulders, and her life was, once again, taking on some sort of purpose. In just over a week, she saw herself back in London, back at Med. school, and with everything back to normal. The only part she wasn't looking forward to, was facing David O'Connor; he had been such a bastard; beating her up, leaving her marooned and penniless, miles from nowhere. She had got away with revenge on Ted Jackson, but could she go through it all again with O'Connor? Any meeting with him was still light years away. Perhaps she could have Professor Wilding throw him out of Med. school, or something! Anyway, she still had to get home. David O'Connor would have to wait.

"Are you okay, Helen?" Mike was suspicious of her buoyant mood. What was going on?

"I've never felt better Mike!"

Four young men came into the restaurant shortly after opening.

"Yes, chaps. What can I get you?"

"Four Bud Lights. Thanks."

Helen was still humming when she returned with the four opened bottles and glasses.

"Say, you don't have three more friends like you out the back, do ya?"

"Sorry guys. I'm unique!" Helen was relishing the flattering attention. It had been a while since she felt relaxed with her sexuality. 'Revenge must have had some healing properties,' she thought.

The four men stayed about an hour, and although they didn't eat they left Helen a huge tip. She made a mental note to be extra nice to everyone, if it meant more money!

Leon Jones was chatting to a couple at the bar. When he saw Helen go into the kitchen for a break, he excused himself, and followed her. "Helen, you have worked real hard, lately, it must be time for you to have some time off. Mary says she can do tomorrow, either lunch or dinner, so just say the word!"

"Thanks, Leon, but I'd rather work both shifts, if that's alright. I'm busy saving up for something!"

Leon was staggered at her single-mindedness. "Okay, suit yourself."

Helen walked out to the restaurant, and a man sitting at a table on the balcony was beckoning her. She took her pad and pencil out to him. He was sitting with his wife and two children. "Hi, folks. You need some menus?"

"Oh I think we know what we want already."

Helen wrote down the orders, and before going back into the main restaurant she gently tousled the blond hair of the youngest child. 'That's got to be worth a couple of dollars on the tip!' she thought, callously.

She swung through the doors, still feeling on a high. She strutted over to the kitchen hatch and shouted the order through to Mike, at the same time piercing the sheet of paper from her pad onto one of the hooks, then turned the contraption until the paper was on Mike's side of the hatch. It was as if she had been a short order waitress all her working life. To her constant surprise she really enjoyed it!

"Excuse me. Miss?" Someone called out to her from a side table. Helen turned towards the voice, still smiling as she thought of the larger tips. "Yes, sir?"

Suddenly, she was looking at the handsome face she knew so well. Martin Tyler smiled and waited for her to walk right up to his table.

"Will you join me for a drink?" There was nothing Helen wanted more.

"I...I'm sorry. I can't. I'm working. Can I get you something?" She knew her voice was sounding different, almost croaky, but she hoped he would just assume it was like that all the time.

"I'll have a lemon tea, please."

"Anything to eat?" Her voice was getting back to normal.

"No thanks. I'd love some of your prawns and hushpuppies, but I have to watch my cholesterol!"

"Of course, how *are* you?" Helen found herself sitting down on the seat opposite him, waiting for his response.

"Oh, I'm absolutely great. That's why I'm here now. I just *have* to take you out. I won't take 'no' for an answer!" He placed his elbow on the table, rested his chin in his hand and just smiled at Helen.

"I... I don't know.." Of course she did.

"How about I call round tomorrow at eleven? I have to go back to the hospital for the results of some tests, and I'd be really grateful if you could drive me. My rental car was returned when I got sick. Then, perhaps we could have a picnic. I love picnics!"

Helen leant her elbow on the table as well. "So do I!"

"So, do you think you can get the time off, tomorrow?"

Helen stood up and pushed the chair back tidily, "Yes I can, I must just go and see Leon. Till tomorrow, then," and she skipped away to tell Leon she would, now, be taking him up on his offer.

Martin Tyler moved to one side, caught Leon's attention before Helen reached him, and smiled as he winked.

Chapter Thirty-Nine

Helen had trouble sleeping again.

She got up early and spread all her clothes on her bed. For the next hour she dressed, undressed and changed.

She finally settled on a very simple combination of T-shirt and shorts. 'What if he's smart?' Then she changed again, but remembered feeling like a hooker the last time she wore the short skirt, and changed back. 'This is ridiculous!' she thought. 'He is taking me out just for a simple 'thank you' picnic, just calm down!'

She was in the bathroom studying the red rash on her neck when Martin Tyler knocked on her door. It was five to eleven. She cursed his punctuality; maybe she might have got rid of her nervous rash in another five minutes!

She put her head down, spotted the slightest hint of a double chin, cursed again, thought, 'sod it!' and just went and opened the door.

Martin Tyler was wearing navy blue knee length shorts and a white Ralph Lauren open necked shirt with the cuffs turned back to just below the elbow. His Timberland loafers were immaculately clean, and Helen felt a real scruff as she thought about her pink T-shirt which was bought for its cost, not its looks. 'What do you expect from three T-shirts for $10? God, how embarrassing!'

"Morning, Helen. You look lovely!" Helen was impressed that he knew her name.

She drove out of the restaurant car park like a learner. She had not felt this nervous since her first interview with the great Professor Wilding. Martin put his briefcase and mobile phone on the back seat, Helen thought he wanted to keep his wits about him in the front.

"Thanks for doing this, Helen. Hopefully, the hospital bit won't take long."

"What are they going to do?" The words were out before she realised how nosy that must have sounded.

"Well, they need to do another cholesterol check to see if it has improved since the attack. It *was* sky-high."

The enormous red-brick building was up ahead on the right of the road. Just before turning into the grounds of Carteret General Hospital Helen took note of a line of shops. Among them she saw a shoe outlet, a gun shop, a sports shop, and a Winn Dixie supermarket. "Listen, I think I'll get some things for the picnic over there while you're busy. Any thing in particular you fancy?"

"Nope. Go steady on the cheese and butter, though!" he said, light-heartedly. He took out a hundred dollar bill and gave it to Helen when she pulled up outside the entrance. "If you park somewhere over by those trees, I'll find you." He smiled and got out of the car. Leaning back through the open window, he said: "Don't forget some champagne. It's very good for cholesterol you know!"

Helen smiled and drove back out to the nearby shops. There was a present for Ted Jackson she needed to buy. He must still be in this hospital. She promised herself that this would be the last time she would ever give him so much as a second thought.

When she got back to the hospital car park, she found a shady space by the trees. There was no sign of Martin yet, so she got out, carrying a brown paper shopping bag, turned over at the top. Nervously, she headed for the main entrance. There were lots of people milling about. She got lost in the crowd.

On a wall-mounted board was a list of all the wards. She studied it for a while, then walked towards the elevator.

The desk on the men's surgical ward was manned by three uniformed women. Two of them were busy talking on the phone, the third, a young woman, was writing. Helen went up to the girl and put the bag on top of the counter.

She looked up and smiled at Helen. "Hello. Can I help you?"

Helen felt the rash on her neck come back.

"Er, yes. I believe an old friend is in here. I have something for him."

"What name was it?"

"Jackson. Ted Jackson." Helen was almost whispering.

The receptionist studied the list in front of her.

"Ah, yes. Here we are. But visiting hours are..."

"I don't want to see him, I just want him to have this."

She pushed the paper bag nearer the girl who took it and looked inside. And smiled.

"Sure. I'll see he gets this right away. Who shall I say brought it?"

"Oh. Don't worry about that. I think he'll guess!"

Helen walked away, exhilarated. Ted Jackson could now be forgotten, she hoped.

Helen got back to the beetle just before Martin Tyler arrived.

"How was it?" Martin knew she really was concerned.

"Just great! It's coming down. They're pleased. So am I."

'Me too,' thought Helen.

The girl in the white uniform went to Ted Jackson's room. She was carrying the brown paper bag. The metal cage under the blanket to keep it off his wound was still a source of amusement to all the female staff. Smiling, she handed him the package. "Look what you've got! Someone loves you!"

Puzzled, Jackson unfurled the top of the bag and looked inside.

The brown paper was damp and cold. "Who the hell gave you this?"

"An attractive young lady, that's who! She had the sweetest accent I've ever heard. I don't think she could have been American. You sly ol' Dog!"

Jackson's face turned into a hard frown; all the women he had screwed had never been outside of North Carolina. He wouldn't describe any of them as 'attractive'.

And then he remembered the barefoot girl with the torn brown blouse.

The young nurse was still smiling at the bulge over his groin as she left the room.

Jackson lifted the brown tub of Ben & Jerry's ice cream out of the limp bag.

It was 'Coffee Toffee Crunch'; the flavour he always kept in his freezer at home.

Chapter Forty

Martin Tyler led the way to a clump of wind-swept trees among the sand dunes. He was carrying a brown paper grocery bag and his mobile phone. Helen was close behind with a bottle of American champagne and two plastic glasses.

This end of the beach was deserted. Helen looked back along the curve of the coastline towards Atlantic Beach, thinking she might make out the restaurant which had been her home these last couple of weeks. Everything was lost in a salty haze.

The waves were louder and whiter up here as they folded over the submerged rocks. The miles of pale, warm sand had turned into patchy dunes between the grey crags. Helen, strangely, found the hostile surroundings more tranquil. Maybe it was the company she was keeping.

Martin was walking from one dune to the next, trying to get a better reception on his mobile phone: "....so please, *no* calls for at least the next two hours. And only in an emergency. I'm on my mobile. Okay, that's great. Thanks Marcie. Bye."

He slapped down the aerial and tossed the phone onto the sand next to where Helen was sitting.

They both thought the food tasted wonderful: cold breast of chicken pulled off the bone, succulent tomatoes, crisp endive leaves, and a fresh loaf of crusty bread that was still warm. When that was all gone, the two of them ate over a pound of seedless white grapes.

It was all washed down with the chilled champagne.

"So, what's your story, Helen Slater? I know your name, but I'd like to know a lot more."

The food, champagne, and company had made Helen feel calm, happy and at peace with the world. She lay back on a patch of sand with her hands under her head, and started telling this virtual stranger everything! Her grandmother, medical school, David O'Connor, the trip to America, and most painful of all, Ted Jackson.

Martin Tyler was leaning against a large boulder in the sand, his hand within touching distance of Helen. He listened in silence to Helen's account of her young life, fascinated, and honoured that she had chosen to share it with him. It was clear that Leon Jones knew nothing about his new waitress, other than she was a good worker, but Martin had known there had to be more to her. Helen felt her eyes well up with tears. It was awful reliving the horrors, but the tears were also from relief that she had been able to get so much out in the open.

Martin gently touched her forehead and started to stroke her hair. The tears kept coming, and soon Helen was sobbing out loud. Like a child with a cut knee, she instinctively turned towards the source of comfort; she dried her eyes on the white Ralph Lauren shirt, Martin's arms were encasing her, safely. This felt so right.

Still holding each other, they made themselves comfortable, lying on the sand. They didn't talk. Neither wanted to move. Soon Helen fell asleep. Martin held her, tenderly.

When Helen woke up, she thought she had been dreaming. She was still in Martin's arms. He too had dozed off. She could handle dreams like this.

"Martin, I'm sorry about, you know…"

"Sshhh…Don't say a word." He began stroking her hair again. Helen remembered David O'Connor; apart from sex for the sake of sex, she couldn't bear the thought of him touching her, but here she was with a man she hardly knew, and she was loving his caress. She never wanted him to take his arms away.

Helen leant against his chest, and they both looked out to sea. "I hate to break this up, but I have to do some work this afternoon. Would you like to have another picnic tomorrow?"

Helen didn't want this one to end, but she didn't belong here. London was her home. She had to focus on going home to get qualified as a doctor. The last thing she needed was a tie; a reason to make her return to London painful. "I'd love to."

They tidied up their picnic site and headed back to the faithful little car. Half a bottle of champagne mixed with sunshine, and nervous tension, not to mention severe lack of sleep over the last few nights, had made Helen feel exhausted. She was looking forward to a siesta on her bed before the dinner shift at the restaurant.

"Do you fancy a coffee? 'Cos there's a place down there." Martin was pointing through the car window to a hot dog trailer parked on a busy part of the beach.

"Good idea!" Helen pulled up just off the road.

"How do you take your coffee, Helen?"

"White, no sugar." She watched him walk away towards the trailer, smiling to herself; she had just told this man her entire life history, warts and all, and he didn't even know her well enough to know how she liked her coffee!

He was still in line behind a middle-aged couple when Helen heard a ringing noise from behind her. It was his mobile phone. She got out of the car and shouted after him, but her voice was drowned out by the roar of the waves. She remembered him saying. ' *..only in an emergency..*' so she picked the phone up, pulled up the aerial and pressed the green button. "Hello?"

"Yes, who's this?" It was a woman's voice on the other end.

"My name is Helen Slater, I..."

"I thought this was Martin Tyler's number!"

"Yes it is, but..."

"I need to speak to him now."

"Yes but he's..."

"Look. Just give him a message, will you? Tell him to call me at home, straight away."

"Home, right. Er...home where?"

"His home in New Orleans of course!"

"Oh okay Who shall I say called?"

"Mrs. Tyler."

*

Helen stared at the black plastic box in her hand. She had always hated the posers in London, constantly talking on their mobile phones. Now she knew why; they were nothing but trouble!

She reflected on the picnic; Martin Tyler had told her nothing about *his* life. She had spilled out almost everything to him, and he didn't even have the guts to tell her he was married!

She found herself experiencing a new emotion; jealousy. That was after the emotions of anger, frustration and betrayal had moved aside. In the past she had almost willed David O'Connor to go off with another woman. She had certainly never given it a fleeting thought if he was late, or seen drinking with a girl in the student bar. She simply didn't care about him, or them, as a couple. But now, the thought of Martin Tyler having a wife made her feel empty and lost. Helen had never believed in love at first sight. Before a few days ago she had never believed in love. 'Still,' she tried desperately to console her shattered feelings, 'it's better to find out now than after something happened. Because it surely would have happened!'

Martin clambered up the grassy bank holding two lidded polystyrene cups. He smiled as he passed them both through the open window to Helen. "I've got half the beach in my shoes!"

He bent down, took them off, and tipped out all the sand.

As he got in the car, Helen looked at his left hand. 'Not only is he married,' she thought, '..but he is scheming enough not to wear a wedding ring.' She had always been suspicious of men who chose not to wear wedding rings; why couldn't they face up to the responsibility of being married? They would surely be the ones to speak up soon enough if their wives swanned around, ringless. 'Any husband of mine will have to wear one.

That's if I ever get married!'

She took a deep breath. "There was a call for you. It was your wife." She looked straight ahead as she spoke.

"My *wife*? Couldn't have been–"

'Oh thank God!'

"–she would *never* call me at work!"

Helen started to lose the grip around her cup and steadied it with the other hand.

"What did she say?"

Helen thought the painful lump in her throat was going to pop right up if she wasn't careful. She took some more deep breaths.

"She said could you call her at home in New Orleans, straight away."

"New Orleans?"

"Well? That's where you live, don't you?"

"Sure! I do. But my wife lives with a lawyer in Alabama. My *ex*-wife, that is. What made you think it was her who called me?"

"She said she was at your home, and her name was Mrs. Tyler. I suppose you're going to tell me now that she's your mother!"

Martin began to laugh. "She *is* my mother!"

Helen knew he was telling the truth. She wanted to fall through one of the rust holes and disappear! She covered her eyes with her hand and smiled. Martin was flattered that it bothered her.

"I suppose you're going to tell me that she sounded like an old dragon. Short-tempered and nasty? Yep. That's Mom!"

Helen just smiled.

"I better give the old girl a call. She's staying at my house while her place is being re-decorated. I'm kinda sorry I offered now; I bet the phone call was to bitch about something or other! Those poor workmen. She makes their lives a hell!"

"So how long have you been divorced?" She couldn't help herself.

"Oh, let's see. Coming up four years."

Helen was driving back on the Atlantic Beach road, intrigued by the divorce.

"So, who divorced who?" She *had* to know.

"Say, what is this?" Martin was still smiling, amazed that his private life should produce so much interest. "If you really want to know I divorced her."

Helen was itching to make him go on. He did. "I travel a lot – as you know – and, I guess we didn't really have that much in common. It was one of those student romances; we met at LSU. and were married the same week we graduated."

"What's LSU?" She needed all the details.

"Louisiana State University. Anyhow, life went marching on, I started working at Cajun Kitchen headquarters in Baton Rouge as a marketing executive, and my wife got a job as a legal secretary in New Orleans. I guess we drifted apart, I didn't pay her enough attention, and the inevitable finally happened: I got home off a trip a day ahead of schedule, thinking I would surprise her, and my God, how I surprised her! She was making love to her boss; the senior partner in her law firm."

Helen slowed down as she became aware of familiar buildings. It was only another couple of minutes to the restaurant, but it sounded like there was more than a couple of minutes worth of story left.

"So what did you do?" She thought about Bob Eckhart finding someone in bed with his wife.

"Well, he grabbed his clothes and took off, she was crying and stuff, and I got undressed, and got into my bed. I didn't say a word to either of them. I didn't have to! But you know what the worst bit was? The bed was still warm from where he'd been lying.

"I'll never forget that feeling as long as I live!

"I didn't love her, granted, but my pride was hurt. You know what I mean? She shouldn't have done that to me!"

It was Helen's turn to comfort him. She placed her hand on his knee and patted it a couple of times as if to say, "There, there. It's alright now."

They were almost at the restaurant, she had forgotten about taking Martin back to his hotel.

"That's okay, Helen, because I have to see Leon, anyway. Hence the briefcase. We've got to tidy up a few loose ends."

"Good, maybe *you* could ask him if I can have tomorrow off!"

Helen steered the car into her usual space, thinking she better not ask him any more questions. She wondered what his ex-wife's name was. Perhaps it would be best if she didn't know.

"Don't forget to call your mother. What's her first name?" It wouldn't hurt to know hers!

"Louise."

"That's my middle name!" she said, proudly.

Chapter Forty-One

Helen woke up feeling as happy and refreshed as she could remember. As she showered she thought about the day before; she imagined the look on Jackson's face when he saw the ice cream tub just like the one he kept his money in, the money she stole. She was smiling as she pictured his penis with a hole in it. Or maybe the end of it had been blown off! She was laughing out loud as she lathered her hair with shampoo.

Her thoughts turned to Martin Tyler and how relaxed she felt in his company. She remembered feeling so threatened and jealous when she thought he was married. And then when they parted company, he had given her a simple peck on the cheek. She touched her face as if to bring back the kiss.

Helen had agreed to meet Martin at ten that morning. Leon had happily asked Mary to do Helen's lunch shift; 'Anything to help the business negotiations run smoothly,' he thought.

Helen was not going to be caught out wearing tatty clothes again, so she put on the mini skirt, the sleeveless top, and cotton jacket. 'Not bad!' she thought.

Martin knocked on her door just before ten. He was wearing flip-flops, swimming shorts, and a plain white T-shirt. They looked each other up and down, and burst out laughing. "Come in, Martin. I think I have to change!"

They set of for a walk along the beach. Helen's beach. But now she was happy to share it. They walked in the surf, carrying their sandals, talking about everything.

"How's your mother? Did you call her?"

"Yes. Last night. I was right. She wanted to tell me that the workmen had lost her door key and that she couldn't get in. She knew I had a spare somewhere. By the time I called, they'd found it. Panic over! So tell me. How ya doing? You got pretty upset yesterday – you've been through hell!"

"Oh, I'm fine, thanks. To tell you the truth, it was so nice to get it off my chest. I feel so much better today." He put his arm around her shoulder as they walked. She soon plucked up courage and put her arm around his waist. They were a perfect fit!

After a couple of hours of walking and talking, they both started to get very hungry. "Let's go have some lunch!" Martin led Helen off the beach when he spotted a line of restaurants on the other side of the boardwalk. "We can check out the competition!"

They sat outside at a seafood restaurant. It was a lot grander than Leon's Beach Hut along the beach, and Helen was glad she was not paying for it.

The lunch was wonderful. Helen ate grilled salmon steak with new potatoes and a crisp green salad. Martin had the fish soup which was a meal in itself. "You know, they said my attack was brought on by too much cholesterol, and too much stress. I guess my job is pretty stressful. But these last couple of days I've felt so relaxed, and happy. And the work is getting done just the same. Thank you for that. I've really enjoyed being with you." Helen sensed finality in his words.

"Yes. Me too. But you don't have to go home just yet? Do you?"

Martin looked down, and shook his head slightly. "I'm going to have to go in the next couple of days. They want me back in Baton Rouge. I've strung it out as long as I dare. Besides, you've got a Med. school waiting! You're going back soon, aren't you?"

Helen looked down now. "Mmm. I think I've got enough for a plane ticket. Just!"

Martin took a credit card out of the inside pocket of his swim shorts. After he had signed for lunch, they walked through the restaurant to the road. He had asked the waiter to call a cab for them, and as they sat outside on a wall, waiting, they were silent. As the cab pulled up in front of them, he smiled at Helen, and they both got into the back seat. "Driver, do you know of a shopping mall nearby? I need to buy some clothes."

'You can get a lot of shopping done in a couple of hours,' Helen thought. Martin had bought her a shirt, two blouses, a pair of jeans, a pair of shoes, a bag, and a bunch of flowers. Helen had made all the right noises, but he had insisted on all the purchases. "I know money's tight, right now. You can pay me back when you're a rich doctor!" Helen wondered if he really had the intention of staying in touch.

They got another cab back to Leon's. Martin did not get out. He kissed Helen on the cheek. "I'll call you tomorrow?" Helen smiled and nodded. She got out, and watched the cab disappear out of the restaurant car park.

There was an hour or so before the evening rush started. Helen lay on her bed, looking at the fresh flowers standing in a coke bottle. 'Another peck on the cheek?' she thought. 'What was the matter with him? What was the matter with *me*? Doesn't he fancy me? Is he gay? Yesterday I though he was sweet for not trying anything on. Today, he's driving me nuts!'

She went round and round in circles. 'Let's face it,' she told herself, 'he's going to go back to New Orleans, and I'm going to go back to London, and the only time I will actually have kissed him on the lips, will be when I was pumping air into his lungs!'

Helen worked hard all evening. She had a pocket full of tips, and there was a nice crowd of people in tonight. Mike was quiet, Rita offered a hand, and Leon was his usual, charming self. Probably more so. "So, how is Mr Tyler?" he asked.

"He's fine, thanks Leon." He couldn't think of anything else to say on the subject, and finally just said, "Oh good, good." He really wanted to know if the deal with Cajun Kitchens was about to go through. Maybe Martin had told her.

It had been a long day. Helen was sitting outside drinking coffee with Rita while Leon counted the evening's takings at the bar.

Even from the balcony, the two women heard a knock at the locked glass doors.

They both looked through and saw Leon let Martin Tyler in. He came straight out to the balcony. "I didn't feel like waiting till tomorrow!"

Helen left half a cup of coffee on the table, said good night to the Joneses, and left with Martin. Leon and Rita smiled at each other without saying a word.

"Do you want to come back to my hotel for a night cap?"

'You bet,' Helen thought. '*At last!*'

"Yes, okay"

She got the keys to the beetle and left her apron on her bed.

Helen noticed two slats of the kitchen venetian blind part as they walked out to the car. 'Poor Mike.'

Martin's hotel room was very tidy. She wasn't surprised.

He poured two beers, and sat down on a cane chair, as Helen took hers and sat cross-legged on the queen-sized bed.

They talked into the small hours. Helen's eyes began to close. It was obvious he was not going to make any moves after all.

"I suppose I better get back. I'm quite tired." She stood up and picked up her car keys from the desk. Martin made no attempt to stop her.

Finally she could stand it no longer. "What's with you?" she shouted, her hands on her hips.

"What do you mean?" He stood up, concerned at her outburst. "What do I mean? I mean *this... you.. nothing*! I've been crying out for you to touch me, and I suppose you were getting ready to give me another peck on the cheek!"

Martin was dumbstruck. Slowly, his face dissolved into a grin, and then he threw his head back and laughed out loud.

Helen was puzzled. He wouldn't stop laughing. She was getting irritated with him. "What's so funny?" He was weak with laughter, while Helen got more and more annoyed. "Okay, what's the joke?"

Martin at last regained control and returned to smiling. He walked over to Helen and rested his hands on her shoulders. "What an idiot I've been!" Helen wasn't about to disagree. "After you told me about your past, and those guys who did such terrible things to you, I thought I just *couldn't* come on to you. I thought you'd just *hate* a man touching you. God, I *wanted* to. So bad!"

Before she knew it, they were embracing. He kissed her forehead, tenderly. Then his lips moved down. They felt soft on hers. She had imagined this moment; it was better than the dream. He stroked her hair as they kissed. As one, they moved towards the bed. They lay side by side, kissing, caressing. She felt his hardness. It excited her. She pressed herself closer. His hands gently explored her body. Touching and stroking. Soon they were both naked. His mouth was kissing her neck. He moved down her body. Her pert nipples became moist as his tongue rolled round one, then the other. She was squirming with ecstasy. Her body was ready for him. She stroked the contours of his lean and muscular back as still he moved down. She didn't think it was possible for someone to give her so much pleasure. And then he was inside her. The gentle rhythmic movements brought waves of pleasure. He felt her hard nipples stroking his chest. He had never been so turned on by anyone before. He forced himself to slow down. To climax now would be such a waste. He never wanted this to end. They lay still. She felt his throbbing. Sex had never been so enjoyable for her. Then the gentle thrusts began again. Faster, and deeper. She wanted to cry out with pleasure. Her body filled with a wonderful tension she had never felt before. Everything was so intense.

And then it was over. He rested on her soft body. She felt his cheek against hers. It was warm and glowing. Their hearts were beating fast and loud. She never wanted to forget this moment. She would never forget his touch. His kiss. His body.

When he had caught his breath he lay by her side. He reached for her hand and squeezed it, gently. As he shut his eyes to sleep Helen lay still, enjoying the warm, satisfied feeling. How could she give all this up? Was he still going to leave her? Would she ever see him again?

She slowly wriggled her hand out from his grip, and then picked up her clothes to get dressed.

It was late. She should be getting back.

Helen looked at him as he slept.

She put her clothes neatly on a chair, picked his up and put them on the same chair, and then carefully slipped between the sheets next to his warm body.

*

The bright sunlight streaming through the sheer curtains woke Helen. Martin's arm was draped across her naked body. He was still fast asleep. She lay still watching the abstract reflections of swaying leaves dance on the ceiling. She thought how restful and serene it looked. But then, anything would look good this morning. She studied his handsome face. Her mind went back to a few hours earlier; she felt a stirring in her loins as she remembered the sex. Up until now, she had thought that sexual chemistry between two people was something that only happened in magazine short stories. Never to real people. Never to people like her. She looked at his tanned, hairless chest gently moving up and down. It made her feel uneasy when she remembered his attack. When it was deathly still. 'Oh God!' she thought, 'I hope all that exertion last night didn't do him any harm!'

He let out a sigh, turned over, and carried on sleeping.

Helen quietly got out of bed and tip-toed into the bathroom.

She shut the door, so as not to wake him, and ran herself a deep, hot bath. She let the water come right up to her neck, as she closed her eyes and once again relived the night of passion. It amazed her how easy sex had been with him; after Ted Jackson she had honestly felt that she could never, ever let a man touch her. Be intimate with her. God forbid, have sex with her. But Martin had steered her through. This was all happening at the wrong time; he had to go in one direction, she the other, with a whopping great ocean in between! She contemplated the future without him. She couldn't afford to lie there any longer; her thoughts would get too painful. Grabbing a white bath towel, she wrapped it around herself and went to get her clothes from the chair in the bedroom. Martin was standing by the counter in a towelling bath robe, emptying two sachets of coffee into cups. "Good morning! Did you sleep okay?" He walked over to her wet body and kissed her on the forehead.

"Mmm. Out like a light!" She brushed past him towards the chair. Martin suddenly grabbed her arm and pulled her back towards him. Holding her tightly, he pressed his lips against hers. She felt his eager body. Her towel dropped to the floor as she opened the gap in his robe, stroking his chest as they kissed. The robe slid off his shoulders as the two lovers fell onto the bed. Helen was on top of him, her long brown hair dripping water into his face.

Astride him, she thought about his heart. "Should you be doing all this? I mean, in your condition?" He smiled as he pulled her down onto him, "I'm in good hands!"

They made love until Helen's hair was almost dry.

They lay under the covers holding each other tenderly.

"You will say if I'm rushing you, won't you?"

"You're not rushing me, Martin. I've never wanted anything so badly!"

He gave her a little squeeze, then groped around by the side of the bed feeling for the bathrobe. "Ready for that coffee, now?"

While Martin saw to the coffee, Helen filled the bath again. She emptied a hotel spa bath sachet into the steaming water.

"Do you want your coffee in the bathroom Helen?"

"Oh. Yes, okay," She paused, then hoped that what she was about to say wouldn't make her sound like a tart, "You can join me, if you like."

Martin didn't answer.

Helen sank down through the clouds of bubbles; the piping hot water took her breath away. Martin walked into the bathroom with two coffee cups. Without saying a word, he put them on the floor by the bath, took his robe off, and stepped in behind her. She lay between his legs, leaning against his chest.

She never thought she could be this intimate with anyone. Sex was one thing, bathing was far more personal.

Martin ordered two full American breakfasts on room service. They were both famished.

"So, what do you think of Cajun Kitchen food?" He took a huge bite out of a sausage.

"To be honest, I've never tried it."

"What? You traitor!" he said jokingly. "You might have to get used to it, they're thinking of opening branches in Europe."

"You're kidding!"

"No I'm not. The US extension program has been such a success, the MD wants to go world-wide. He has already been to Europe on a fact-finding trip. Well, that's what he told us! The gossip machine reckons he just fancied a vacation on expenses."

"Where in Europe?"

"Don't know. But his trip took him to London, Paris and Milan. The fact that he is a tennis nut and opera lover, *and* that he took his wife, has nothing to do with anything."

"What on earth are you talking about?"

"Well, he just happened to be in London for Wimbledon, Madame Butterfly was on at La Scala the next week, and his wife is French, and it was coming up to their twenty-fifth wedding anniversary." He smiled as he shrugged his shoulders.

"Oh. That's rotten. If he really did start up in Europe, you could come and be based in London, couldn't you? Do the same thing there as you're doing here!" She had it all sorted.

"I wish, but don't hold your breath!"

The breakfast trolley had no more than a few crumbs left by the time they were through eating.

"Helen. I have to leave today." He could not bring himself to look at her as he spoke. She felt her cheeks flush as a searing shot of panic coursed up her body like a hot iron. She knew this moment was always around the corner, but it didn't hurt any less when it actually arrived. "I see." She didn't see it at all! Why ruin this? Why spoil everything?

When it finally came, the last embrace was painful. Helen broke away first, her tear-filled eyes were obscuring his handsome face, the lump in her throat made it impossible to speak. There were no more words left.

When she left his room she didn't look back, she just ran towards the trusty beetle, clutching the piece of hotel note paper which had a New Orleans address scribbled on it.

Martin went over to the window, parted the sheer curtains, and watched the lime green car drive out of the hotel grounds.

Chapter Forty-Two

Debbie-Mae kicked off her open-toed sandals and lay back on the brown velour sofa. *Wheel of Fortune* was getting to the exciting bit; she would imagine being the winner of the Ford Bronco every night, even though she had never ever guessed the final answer. It couldn't hurt to dream.

Bob Eckhart was in the bedroom tightening the last screws on the new self-assembly bed base.

"Bobby. Git me a soda."

Bob put the screwdriver on the floor and walked to the kitchen. He took out a bottle of diet Pepsi and hinged off the cap with the wall-attached bottle opener.

"Here ya go, Hon."

She reached up for it without removing her gaze from the television. She said nothing. Bob went back into the bedroom.

Wheel of Fortune finished. Debbie-Mae was bored.

"Bobby. Are we gettin' a take-out tonight?" In other words she wasn't going to cook.

Bob, slightly panting from heaving the new mattress onto the bed-base, walked over to the sofa with his hands on his slim hips.

"Git your purse. I'm takin' you out for dinner."

The cream-coloured car pulled up in the half empty car park of 'Al's Bar and Grill'. The neon Budweiser sign in the window was flickering and buzzing. It needed a new tube.

Of the dozen people inside, the Eckharts knew eight of them. The juke box was loaded with Country and Western songs. Debbie-Mae loved Country and Western. She knew all the dance steps. Bob hated dancing.

Bob sat facing the bar, drinking his beer from the bottle. Debbie-Mae pressed her back against the brass rail and watched a couple dance on the tiny dance space. "Bobby, let's dance!"

"Hell, No! I'm drinkin'!"

Songs by Eddie Rabbit and Garth Brooks shared the juke box. Debbie-Mae's feet were itching.

The Eckhart's ate their steak meals sitting at the bar.

A tall, well-built man in his thirties walked over to them. He was wearing a large, black cowboy hat, checked flannel shirt, skin-tight faded blue jeans, and shining black cowboy boots.

"Hi, Bob. How's it goin' at the gas station?" He slapped Bob between the shoulder blades, making him catch his breath as the last mouthful of well-done T-bone went down.

"Tommy!" He stood up, beaming a genuine smile and shook the cowboy's hand eagerly. "...Great to see ya!"

Debbie-Mae looked at the man. All she saw was Garth Brooks. "Tommy, this is my wife, Debbie-Mae."

The cowboy took her hand in his, and kissed it, looking her in the eye the whole time. "That's a pretty name for a pretty lady!" Debbie-Mae smiled shyly, and straightened her back. Her bosom rose like two buoys in the sea.

"Hon. Tommy and I go way back. He used to be manager at the gas station. Hell, he got me my job!"

Debbie-Mae smiled. "Used to be? What are you doing now, Tommy?" She spoke from her chest.

"I'm area manager now. I have like six gas stations under my control. I keep things ticking over. I know who's where, what's what. That kinda thing."

Bob had bought Tommy a beer, and thrust the bottle into his hand. "Cheers!"

The Rest Room by Garth Brooks started to play. Although a slow number, it was Debbie-Mae's favourite Country song. She gasped and looked longingly at the juke box.

"Do you mind if I ask your wife to dance?"

"You go for it, Tommy."

The cowboy took her hand and helped her off the bar stool. Bob finished his beer as they walked to the dance area. Three other couples were already dancing.

Debbie-Mae fitted snugly under the shadow of the huge hat. She came up to the cowboy's shoulders. She liked big men.

He was careful not to hold her too close. He was aware of her breasts pressed against his stomach. He looked over to her husband

and smiled, aware that his brow was getting very sweaty under the black felt.

The song was almost over. They would have to go back to the bar. The cowboy bent his head, aware that Bob couldn't see his mouth.

"Debbie-Mae, it's been over a month! When am I goin' to see you again? This is drivin' me crazy Babe!"

Debbie-Mae turned while dancing so that her mouth was shielded from her husband's stare.

"Soon, Darlin'. Real soon!"

Bob and Debbie-Mae drove home along the swamp road in silence. It was almost midnight. Bob's week of unpaid leave was almost up. Tomorrow night he would be back at work. Safe in the knowledge that Ted Jackson would no longer pose a threat he knew things between him and his wife would be just great from now on. Debbie-Mae was looking forward to the cowboy; he always had been a close second to Ted.

Suddenly overcome with a strong, lustful urge, Debbie-Mae reached across to her husband's groin, and squeezed. Bob flinched uncomfortably, "Not in the car. Stop that!"

"But Bobby. Don't you remember how we used to do it in the car every night?"

"That was a long time ago. We weren't married then."

"So? Why does the fun have to stop just because it's official? I *need* you to touch me. To hold me. Show me you're a man.."

Bob glared at her. Was that a dig?

"... I'm sorry Bob. I didn't mean that."

He decided to let it go, unchallenged. He had his wife back all to himself. That was the important thing. "I'm sorry, Hon. I've never been much good at this 'romance shit'. It's just not me!" He lifted her arm out of his lap and plonked it back in hers. He kept a tight grip on the steering wheel.

After three years of trying for a baby, tests had finally proved that the problem was all Bob's. Debbie-Mae had always enjoyed her men firing on all cylinders. When Bob found out he was firing blanks, he lost all interest in the mechanics of sex, with his wife anyway. What was the point?

Fortunately, he never heard the standing joke going around the lumber yard, just before he quit:

"What's the difference between Bob and Debbie-Mae Eckhart?"
"Answer: Debbie-Mae has a higher sperm count."

Chapter Forty-Three

Helen recognised the young woman at the door. It seemed like an eternity had past since the last time she saw her. Pregnant then, and with her blond hair in a pony tail, she still looked the same now, with maybe a few more bags under her eyes.

"Hello. You must be Chrissie. I've brought your car back at long last!"

"Helen, isn't it? Come in."

She led Helen into a chaotic lounge, the fair-haired baby asleep in her arms. "Sit down. If you can find a chair! You want a drink?"

Helen opted for a coke; she didn't see how Chrissie could cope with making tea.

Chrissie gingerly placed the sleeping babe into a very old looking wicker crib, and stepped back silently, almost holding her breath. The baby stayed asleep.

"If you don't mind me saying, you looked shagged out! Are you coping okay?"

"Oh, sure. I wouldn't give Catherine up for the world! But she is hard work! I had no idea!"

"What about Gary? Is he a 'nineties' dad?"

"Gary? *My* Gary? He *thinks* he's God's answer to fatherhood, but in reality if he ends up in the same room as a dirty diaper, he thinks he's done real well!" At least she could still smile about it. "I think he'll make a great dad when she's in her teens. That should give him long enough to get used to the idea!"

The two young women had absolutely nothing in common, except their age, but they still found enough to talk about. Chrissie just enjoyed talking to a human being that could talk back, and Helen was almost envious of her simple, uncomplicated, mapped out life. She wanted for nothing. Helen wanted it all.

"Gary should be back soon. Why don't you stay for dinner?" Helen wondered what on earth they could eat; she had noticed that the fridge was virtually empty when she helped herself to the last coke.

"No, really. Don't go to any trouble."

"It's no trouble. Gary was going to bring home a Chinese take out. He has this friend who runs a restaurant. I'll just give Charlie a call and have him make up a bigger order. No sweat."

Gary arrived home half an hour later, with a bulging brown bag full of Chinese food and a six pack of beer.

The three of them sat on the floor, Chrissie skilfully eating around the baby who had been at her breast for hours, so it seemed. They laughed and joked like old friends. The food was fantastic. The beer was great.

"I'm going back to England tomorrow. I can't tell you how grateful I am; the two of you have been so good to me..." Helen felt the emotions running high.

Gary Koblonski hated seeing a woman 'blubber' and intervened before she got any worse. "So was the car okay? Get you everywhere you needed to go?"

"It was more than okay. I love that car!" She wiped a tear away as they all laughed at her sarcasm.

"You *did* have your driver's licence on you at all times, didn't you?" Gary wasn't smiling anymore.

Helen stared at him long and hard before answering. He *knew* she had nothing when they first met. No passport. Not much money. No shoes. Was this a joke? Or was he really that stupid? Sometimes he seemed too stupid for words. Other times it was as if he knew too much. On the spot, Helen convinced herself that he really was naive, and she was reading too much into it. "What do YOU think?" She smiled.

Helen got off the floor, and looked down at the feeding baby, thinking that she was going to explode if she drank anymore milk!

"You've got yourselves a lovely little girl. You're very lucky! She's beautiful!"

Gary's embarrassment was only upstaged by his pride. He stood up to see Helen out. Chrissie carried on feeding; her full, raw bosom making Helen feel a bit better about her lost chance of motherhood. Helen took a package out of her bag and handed it to her. "It's just a little something for Catherine. And this is for you."

She had taken out another small parcel, and Gary had taken it as Chrissie's hands were full.   .

The baby came unstuck as Chrissie ripped the paper off a little pink dress, milk squirting all over the place. "Ah Gee, that's sweet!" she said as she held the dress up with one hand, while automatically pushing the sucking mouth back onto the milk fountain. Gary unwrapped the other present. It was a small model car. A bright green Volkswagen Beetle.

"I couldn't find one with rust!"

Chapter Forty-Four

Gary dropped Helen back at the restaurant just before midnight. Tomorrow would be her last day in America.

These last few weeks had changed her life so much; she had experienced the worst type of people, and the best.

She lay on her bed in the darkened room that had become home. All her thoughts turned to Martin Tyler. Was becoming a doctor *really* that important? What if she never saw him again? What if she never met anyone like him again? What if he did this every time he is away on a business trip? She imagined dozens of lovelorn women all over America, pining for the handsome businessman who had touched their lives for a few days and then disappeared back to New Orleans! She felt ill.

Morning took forever to arrive. Helen felt exhausted. The bus left for Washington in less than three hours. She could remember once looking forward to this day so much. Now she cursed its arrival.

She took a huge breath and forced herself to get out of bed. There was plenty of room for all her newly acquired belongings in the old shoulder bag which Rita had found in her basement. Helen had felt awful giving them just three days notice, but Rita was as charming and understanding as ever. Leon was simply too preoccupied with his imminent retirement to care.

The deal with Cajun Kitchens was now complete, and Rita and Leon Jones had just five more weeks to wait before the workmen moved in to transform his life's work.

Leon had wanted to see the renovations through, but his wife had wisely persuaded him to leave beforehand, "Let's remember this place as Leon's Beach Hut Restaurant, eh?" So they had decided to pack up early, and they would be heading back to Goldsboro next month.

"Helen, it's eleven o'clock. How ya doing?"

She opened her door to Leon, who was ready to drive her to the bus station. He picked up the dusty bag and led the way out to his car. Rita came down the wooden steps from the restaurant carrying a brown grocery bag rolled over at the top. "Thought you might need some sandwiches for the bus ride, it's a long way."

Helen took the bag but was too emotional to say anything. The middle-aged black woman, and the young English girl hugged like mother and daughter. Eventually, Helen nodded, and smiled through her tears. She got into the car beside Leon.

"Wait a minute, where's Mike?" Helen had already opened her door to go up to the kitchen.

"Oh, he's not coming in to work today. He called in sick." Guiltily, Helen shut the door, thinking what a bitch she had been to poor Mike. She looked back and waved to Rita as she left the car park for the last time.

When they drove past the bright blue water tower, leaving Atlantic Beach behind, Helen was suddenly overcome with all sorts of emotions. The tears rolled silently down her flushed cheeks.

Leon was too much of a gentleman to make her talk, so he just kept his eyes on the road and his thoughts to himself.

Chapter Forty-Five

Mike wouldn't be going in to work today.

He had phoned Leon to say he woke up feeling sick. He stood at the window of his rented room looking at the street below. Mrs. Sanner was vacuuming the hall. She always vacuumed the hall on Tuesdays and Fridays.

Mike walked over to the door and checked that it was locked. The last thing he needed right now was his chatty, nosy landlady barging in to clean his carpet.

He put his hands in the pockets of his shorts and mooched around the room aimlessly. He didn't have many personal possessions in the tidy, spartan, first floor room: a collection of second-hand paperbacks, an ancient portable TV with a horizontal hold problem, and a couple of cheap photo frames.

He would buy more things when he was married. He didn't need anything now, but a home with a wife and maybe a couple of kids – they could buy stuff together. He had read all the books at least twice. He flicked through the newest looking one, but wasn't inspired to read it for the third time. If he put the TV on it would prove to Mrs. Sanner that he was there and she may feel obliged to ask him how he was, and if he wanted to join her for a cup of coffee.

He looked out of the window again. The boarding house was one block removed from the main Fort Macon Road. He could hear the cars above the din of the vacuum cleaner. He sat on the ledge of the open window and stared back into his room. His gaze fell on the wooden photo frame by his bed.

They made such a great couple. She would have made such a pretty bride; her blonde hair, always pulled back in a ponytail, could have been made fancy, with maybe some flowers in it. Mike had the whole thing planned: what she would wear, what he would wear, the reception at Leon's, honeymoon in Hilton Head, he would have

looked for a better paid job, she could have given up working;
everything would have been perfect.

Mike lay on the green candlewick bedspread, holding the photo
frame to his chest.

Maybe he really was sick? A nap might help.

The photo frame fell onto the carpet. Mike woke up with a start.
He had been asleep for three hours. The vacuuming had stopped at
least. He reached down and took one last look at the picture before
placing it back in its place, next to the other frame.

He lay back yawned, and rubbed his eyes into life. Through the
open window he heard the roar of a long-distance bus drive along the
main road. Was Helen on that one, or did she catch the eleven thirty?
She didn't care about him either.

The sun was still burning at six o'clock. He walked along Fort
Macon Road, away from Leon's. It was a toss-up between
MacDonald's or Burger King for dinner. It had been hours since he
last ate. His corpulent stomach was rumbling. Unable to decide, the
fairest thing was to eat in both.

The evening sky was turning the colour of a blueberry muffin.
Mike mingled with the Friday night traffic on the boardwalk.
Everyone was in pairs, or groups. Only Mike was all alone.

He studied the faces of the men he passed; they weren't *all* good
looking, but they managed to have women. Some were a lot fatter
than Mike, and positively ugly, but they still had friends, wives,
lovers.

By ten o' clock he felt he had wasted enough of a good day. If he
got home now he could watch David Letterman through rotating
stripes. Maybe he would spend his savings on a new TV. He didn't
need the money for anything else, anymore.

Mike left the boardwalk to take a short cut through some factory
buildings. It saved walking all the way up to Prince Street, and then
back along the main drag. He knew it came out just a couple of
blocks away from his road. This way he would be back at the
boarding house in less than fifteen minutes.

The alleyway was totally unlit, and it was deserted. The three
storey buildings either side blanked off the last of the day's natural
light.

Mike's footsteps echoed off the shadowy walls. Was this such a
good idea? He thought about turning back and joining the people

walking by the beach, but that would entail even more walking. He must be about half way through by now. He wouldn't cut through here again.

A loud noise, like a freight train, grew behind him. He spun round, startled, to see two youths bearing down on him on roller blades. They reached him in a flash, gliding past either side of a terrified Mike, cursing and gesticulating as they skated by him at high speed. The dark-clad youths circled around each other then swept past Mike again, their high pitched chants bouncing off the brickwork. Overwhelmed with fear, he couldn't move. They laughed at his panic. He felt the rush of wind as they skimmed by him once more, their outstretched padded elbows knocking into his flabby chest. They kept on skating. As soon as he caught his breath, and was sure they weren't looking back at him, he stuck a defiant middle finger up. They were lucky he didn't catch them!

Mike took some deep breaths. He could feel his heart thumping out loud. Those burgers had given him indigestion. The alleyway looked even darker. He could see car lights. A road was just up ahead. He didn't remember this route being so long. Maybe it had always been daylight when he came this way before now. At least he was safe.

There was just one factory block before the road. Mike could even hear voices. People, at last!

As he reached the corner of the last building he saw a car parked by the rear gates. Its lights were on, the engine was running, and two people were standing nearby. A slim black girl aged about twenty, or younger, was trying to pull her arm away from the grip of an older man. He was black with a neat, sculptured, beard, long, straightened hair tied in a ponytail, and heavy gold rings on every finger of both hands. In the sweltering August temperatures, he was wearing a black leather sports jacket, over a black shirt which was open to the waist. More gold jewellery hung around his solid neck. The young girl had on a red leather halter top, and a matching skirt that was so short her panties were clearly visible, even when she stood upright. As she tried to pull away the man's voice turned to a shout. He kept a tight grip of one wrist and started slapping her about the face with his free hand. The girl started to kick him with her high heeled shoes, yelling out obscenities that a young girl just should not know. Mike was horrified by the brutality shown by the big man. The girl didn't stand a chance.

Before Mike had a chance to think whether or not he should get involved, the black man caught sight of him.

"You got a problem?" he sneered at Mike, still holding the wriggling girl with consummate ease.

"Hey. Let her go, for Chrissake!"

"Fuck you!" As if to repay Mike for his meddling, the black man karate-chopped the girl across her stomach. She fell to the ground, winded.

Mike ran towards her. "You bastard!"

He heard a metallic click.

The black man was holding a switch-blade knife.

Mike stopped dead. Now what?

The girl was choking, writhing about in agony. The black man stood over her, but his stare was fixed on Mike. Both men were motionless.

The girl started to crawl away like an injured snake. Her pimp slowly turned and looked at her. Tantalisingly, he let her slither so far, then calmly walked over and kicked her in the small of her back. Without thinking of the consequences, Mike ran and leapt on the leather jacket, punching the persecutor with all his strength. The black man staggered towards the wall, his legs buckling under Mike's weight. He tried to shake him off, but Mike clung on, for all he was worth. Mike felt the wall smash into him. He lost his grip and fell. He tried to stand up as fast as he could. The pimp waited for him to get up. Mike was pinned against the wall. The black man was pressing into him. The sudden, burning pain in his side took his breath away. The black man was looking into his eyes, his right hand buried into Mike's body. He pulled it away. The knife hurt more coming out. Mike went limp. His hands and legs wouldn't work. The pain was unbearable. Determined to stay upright, his body let him down. As he slowly slid down the wall, the black man watched him. The last thing Mike saw was his smiling face.

Mike wouldn't be going in to work tomorrow.

Part Four

Chapter Forty Six

George Wilding was studying the file in front of him.

This was truly a remarkable student, he was thinking, when he heard a timid knock on the solid oak door.

"Come!"

Helen Slater walked in.

She went straight over to the professor, and held out her hand.

"Helen. Lovely to see you. Do sit down."

George Wilding was in his fifties. Although only average height his presence made him appear much taller. Steel grey hair and eyes, his personality was colourful enough. Always an immaculate dresser, Helen was not surprised to see him wearing a dark grey three-piece suit, even though this was the midst of an unusually hot English summer.

"Now then. What are we going to do with you? Thank you for your letter, by the way. Let's hope we can sort this mess out."

"I'm sorry about all this, Professor. Thank you for seeing me."

"You realise you've got a lot of ground to make up. You're not a second year student, wet behind the ears! Two weeks! That's what your leave should have been. I see you should have been attached to a surgical firm for the last month. And you've missed an assessment on pathology and ...microbiology."

He was reading from the file. He peered over his gold, half moon spectacles. If he meant to intimidate her, it worked.

He was sitting on one side of his vast oak desk, Helen the other side on an uncomfortable wooden chair. The strong smell of furniture polish filled the air.

"At the very least you should be required to do another year. And that is only because there were extenuating circumstances, and you let me know. Normally, however, failure to report back after leave would result in instant expulsion."

Helen looked down at her hands. She wanted to cry.

"However," he removed his glasses and leant back in his upholstered chair, "your record thus far has been impeccable. I would hate to see a promising young doctor held back because of unfortunate events. Therefore, I have decided to let you stay in year five – your second MB was the best grade of the year – and provided you give me your assurance that you will move heaven and earth to catch up, you can start your next obstetrics firm on Monday. Under Mr Carr."

Helen looked up and knew now why she had always admired this man so much. She still wanted to cry.

"Thank you, Professor. I won't let you down."

"The only one you'll be letting down is yourself!" He stood up and smiled, "I think you can do it! Good luck!"

Helen had one more nasty piece of business to attend to.

"Professor, this is a bit awkward. As I tried to explain in my letter, the reason I was left marooned in America was David O'Connor: he attacked me and left me by the roadside. Then I discovered he had taken all my belongings; money, plane ticket, passport. I don't think I can face being near him for the next year. Is there anything you can do to keep him away?"

George Wilding slowly walked over to Helen and placed his hand on her shoulder.

"Yes. That must have been absolutely ghastly. I'm amazed the police out there couldn't help you."

"Well, they did. In a way." Helen remembered Gary Koblonski, and the little green car. "So, what do you think you can do about David O'Connor?" Revenge was still top of her agenda.

"I don't think I need do anything, Helen."

She stared at him, horrified. Everything had gone so well up until that point. Surely he could help her. She was counting on it. Revenge was what kept her going, fuelled her desire to survive. She *had* to get even with David O'Connor. This was her plan. And he had turned her down. "But why?" she sounded incredulous.

"I don't think I can do anything. You see, I don't know where he is. Mr O'Connor is no longer a medical student.

"He left."

*

Helen walked out of Professor Wilding's office in a daze. That wasn't part of her plan. David O'Connor shouldn't have left; *she* wanted to have him expelled. He'd ruined everything! She slowly walked along the crowded London streets, oblivious to the noise of the traffic and the army of pedestrians.

'Why did he leave? Where did he go?' Her strides got faster and wider as she became determined to find out.

When she reached a dowdy building, she hesitated before ringing the doorbell of flat five. Eventually a young man opened the door, squinting into the daylight. It was obvious he had just woken up. "Sorry, Trevor. Did I wake you?"

"That's okay. Hi, Helen. Where have you been?"

"It's a long story! Can I come in?"

She followed him into the kitchen. She could almost smell David O'Connor. Then she saw some dried up baked beans in a pan, and remembered that David was always eating beans when he lived here. "Have you seen David?" There was no point wasting time.

"Once. A few weeks ago." Trevor rubbed his eyes and yawned. "Sorry. I've been on nights in A & E all week."

"Oh God, and I woke you!"

"Forget it. What went on between you two? David was really spaced out and jumpy."

"Like I said, it's a long story."

"I take it the holiday didn't cement the relationship?"

"The only things I'd like to see in cement are David O'Connor's feet, before he goes for a swim!"

Trevor laughed, scratched his head, and yawned again. Helen began to yawn as well; it suddenly dawned on her how tired she was; she had only arrived in the UK that morning, and after the stressful meeting with Professor Wilding it was beginning to catch up on her.

"Trevor. Did he say where he was going? Why he's left Med. school?"

"Nope. He came in, collected a few of his things, and said he had to go. He didn't tell me he was quitting. I found out a few days later when we should have started a surgical firm together. He just didn't show up. No one knew anything about it."

"Which consultant were you under?"

"Mr Calloway. He kept asking me if I knew where he was. Just because we shared a flat, doesn't mean I know anything."

They drank coffee, and Helen caught up on the Med. school gossip. David and Trevor had shared a flat for the last three years. Helen had always liked Trevor, probably more than she felt comfortable with, but he had never seemed interested. He had not had a serious girlfriend the whole time he had been a medical student. Helen admired his single-mindedness. She would not be in this mess now had she followed his ethos.

"Do you still have a couple of boxes of my stuff in your cupboard?"

Trevor looked worried. "I don't know. Let's take a look."

Helen yanked out two cardboard packing cases. Rolled up on top of one was a poster. She opened it out, knowing what she was going to see: *The Japanese Footbridge*, by Claude Monet.

"I saw the original in Washington, you know."

Her mind began to dwell on things past. Trevor knew she was upset. "Listen, Helen, have you got your accommodation sorted out? I know the tenancy on your bed-sit ran out."

"Not yet. That was going to be my next little job!"

"Why don't you move in here? I need someone to help with the bills. It's been tough since David left. There's a perfectly good bedroom over there. I was going to advertise it on the notice board, but I haven't got round to it yet."

The idea hadn't occurred to Helen, but she liked it. The flat was small, but it was handy for the hospital, and with a good clean, it should look better. It was, after all, three in the afternoon and she still had no idea where she would stay tonight, let alone the next year. "Okay You're on!"

They each carried a packing case into the second bedroom. David's bedroom.

Helen looked around the grubby, familiar walls.

She felt strange putting her clothes into David's drawers. She pinned the Monet print up on the wall where his poster of a Harley Davidson had been. She looked at the bed. They had made love on that bed. She had probably got pregnant on that bed.

'Oh God! What am I doing?'

When Helen joined Trevor in the lounge, he was busy writing.

"Right. I've drawn up a roster for cooking, vacuuming and washing up. It'll be a bit tricky with us both working shifts, but we can give it a try. Saturday; your turn to wash up!"

Helen flopped into the saggy armchair, smiling. She looked at Trevor; his hair a mess, a two-day old beard, and bare feet.

'I think I'm going to like it here!'

Chapter Forty-Seven

By the end of her first week back, Helen was well into the swing of medical life; it was as if she had never been away. Even being on call on the Obstetrics ward, called at all times of the day and night, hadn't worried her. She thrived on the adrenaline buzz. This was her destiny; she was born to be a doctor. The Obstetrics consultant, Mr Carr, was extremely impressed by her obvious ability. All week long, she had hardly spared a thought for Martin Tyler; maybe he was just an exciting sexual interlude, a wonderful holiday romance.

Helen and Trevor were like ships that passed in the night; when she came home after a ten hour shift, he would be about to start a thirty six hour stint in Accident and Emergency.

His housework roster went to pot; they were both too exhausted to eat, let alone cook. And they were never there long enough to make a mess that needed hoovering up!

On her first real day off, Helen had a couple of things to do. First, she made herself comfortable in the squidgy armchair, with a cup of coffee by her side and a Mars Bar for later. It took her over an hour to write the letter. By the time she put it into an airmail envelope, she had stopped crying.

When she came back after a walk to the post box she couldn't think of an excuse to put it off any longer; she went over to the phone with a piece of paper in her hand.

"Good Morning. Doctor's Surgery." It was a woman with a Northern Irish accent.

"Oh, hello. I'm calling from London, could you put me through to Dr. O'Connor?"

There was a long pause. Thinking she had a bad line, Helen went on, "Hello? Can you hear me?"

"Er. Yes, I can hear you. Who is this?"

"My name is Helen Slater. I know Dr. O'Connor's son, David, and I was hoping he could tell me where I might find him."

Again, there was a long pause. Then the woman said: "Doctor O'Connor is dead. He died last month. The day his son came to see him."

Helen was speechless. She put the receiver back and walked to her armchair, shocked and confused.

She was still sitting in the chair, it had turned dark. Trevor and a friend came into the unlit flat. He turned on the light, startled to see Helen sitting there. Helen hardly registered their presence.

"Hello Helen! This is Peter." Helen just smiled without looking at the two men. She stood up and disappeared into her bedroom. Trevor didn't see her again until the next evening when she came in from the hospital.

The weeks passed by. Helen finished her Obstetrics Firm. She swore she'd scream if she saw another rotund woman with her legs in the air! Her assessment was excellent; Mr Carr was sorry to see her go.

In her free time she wrote letters. She received many. Trevor was intrigued by the constant stream of airmail envelopes, but never quizzed her about them.

She would occasionally meet Trevor and some of the other student doctors in the nearby pub. Some asked her out on dates, but she always refused, saying she had a lot of extra study to do. It was the perfect excuse. Trevor's friend, Peter, was a barman in the pub, and always saw Helen had a drink 'on the house'. Money constantly seemed to be in desperate shortage, so she was keen to stay in his good books.

After a glorious, hot summer, the English winter arrived with a vengeance. Helen had virtually made up all the lost ground, and was well on target to qualifying with flying colours. She had even secured her first real job, at the nearby King George's hospital. Sometimes, on her days off, she would go past the hospital, and then explore the neighbourhood looking for a flat that might suit her better. She couldn't share with Trevor for ever

It was two thirty by the time Helen was walking home after her shift in Intensive Care. She should have been through by ten that morning but she had had to stay with an old lady who had been rushed in the night before with a broken hip and hypothermia. It was thought she had been lying on the floor of her council flat for three days, totally dehydrated and starving; Helen could not believe that this sort of thing was possible in Nineties London. It was only the eighty year old banging on the floor with her fist that made the tenants below call the police. They called the police to complain about the noise.

Helen turned the corner into her street, hunched up, fighting the cold. She was still thinking about the old lady, lying on a freezing floor, in agony. As she neared the flat, Helen saw a man walking away from the front door. It wasn't Trevor, and she hadn't seen Peter for ages. They had obviously fallen out. When she caught up with the stranger she stopped him on the pavement.

"Did you want to see someone at Flat Five?"

The man looked at Helen. He was in his late twenties, wrapped up in a huge skiing anorak, with the fur-lined hood snug around his face. His pale complexion was interrupted by two vivid blue pools. She had only ever seen such blue eyes on one other person.

"Are you Helen?"

Paul O'Connor was three years older than his brother. They could have passed for twins. His thick hair was longer than she had ever seen David's, and maybe he was a little taller.

They drank coffee, both feeling awkward. Helen took the initiative. "How did you find me Paul?"

"I contacted the welfare office at the hospital. David gave me the number years ago in case I had to contact him. The student welfare officer finally told me where you lived. But she wasn't keen on the idea."

Helen could just imagine him flashing his blue eyes, and charming her with his soft Belfast accent; putty in his hands!

"So, why? Why did you want to find me? I haven't seen David for months. Where is he?"

"I have no idea! That's what I came to see you about." He put his coffee cup down, and took out four postcards from his anorak pocket. "These are all from David. One from Glasgow, one from Harrogate, Swindon, and, Truro."

"So he likes to travel!"

Paul handed her the cards. They all said the same thing:

'Dear P, Love, D.'

"That's *it*?"

"I think he's in some kind of trouble. It's as if it's a cry for help. He never gets in touch apart from these postcards, and they don't

168

exactly do much. I got the last one over six weeks ago. I haven't heard from him since."

"Well, I don't know what to suggest. I kind of wanted to see him myself!"

"But I thought you two had broken up? At my father's funeral David said it was over between you two. He was terribly upset by Dad's death, I thought there had to be something else on his mind. I put it down to your break-up. At least he got to see Dad before he died; he was with him at the end!"

"Yes. We had broken up. Not exactly on good terms! I'm sorry about your father. How did he die?"

"A massive heart attack. David tried to resuscitate him, but it was no good. That must have been so hard for him, seeing as he was training to be a doctor, and he couldn't even save his own father's life!"

"Surely he didn't leave medicine just because of that? He only had a year to go."

"I know! That's why I'm convinced there had to be something else troubling him. Are you sure you don't know?"

"Look, Paul. I know he's your brother, but he was a real bastard to me. I won't bore you with the details. But please don't think that I am the one at fault here. If your brother is having nightmares about me, I hope they are really awful!"

"Ooh. You *did* break up on bad terms, didn't you?"

Paul O'Connor did not stay long. His trip had been wasted: He was no nearer finding out where his brother was, what he was doing, or why.

He could see, however, what had attracted him to Helen.

Helen went to bed early. Trevor still wasn't home. She lay awake staring at the darkened ceiling, mulling over the day's events. Without her trying, fate had intervened and taken care of her revenge on David O'Connor.

The matter was now closed.

Chapter Forty-Eight

The car rode over Helen's head. Front wheel. Back wheel.

Her skull had shattered like a peanut shell. Her brains oozed out like thick custard drenched in blood. Her mangled, lifeless body, was now part of the swampy verge. Rotting flesh, devoured by maggots and flies. A crow had pecked out both eyes, wolves had gnawed to the bone. Fragments of brown cotton swayed in the breeze, caught on tall grassy stalks.

"David! What have you DONE?" Patrick O'Connor was lying on the floor, clutching his chest. He looked at his younger son though eyes of horror and despair. His son a murderer.

David O'Connor sat bolt up straight. Terrified.

He had woken up with another dreadful hangover. But he should have drunk more; the more he drank the less he dreamt.

He lay back. His head hit the lumpy hotel pillow with a thud. He wanted to be sick. Swallowing hard usually helped.

The alarm clock radio jolted into life. It was tuned to a local Birmingham station. When he could face opening his eyes, he scanned the room from the safe haven of the bed. a suit jacket was in a crumpled heap next to a chair. His shirt, tie, socks and trousers were scattered across the floor. He was still wearing his underpants. They were sopping wet.

He hauled his leaden legs over the side of the bed. He cradled his throbbing head in his hands, willing the pain to go away. Shuffling into the bathroom, he became aware of his cold backside as the air hit the urine-soaked boxer shorts. It was the same most mornings.

He felt no better after an instant black coffee in the hotel room but at least the urge to throw up had subsided.

David O'Connor spent most of his time on the road; too embarrassed and scared to return to medical school, he was lucky to get this job. He never thought of himself as a salesman, but at least selling drugs to doctors was better than double glazing to suburban housewives. The driving all over the country was okay. At least it kept him occupied, and he didn't have to spend much time in his poky, overpriced digs in Watford. He even got a car with the job; not the Jaguar he had promised himself when he became a consultant dermatologist, but at least the red Peugeot estate was better than the other options the drug firm gave him. And it was brand new. Not that it looked it now; filthy dirty, a crease in the passenger door, and forty thousand miles on the clock. He had only had it six months.

The worst aspect of the job, by far, was being forced to accept the smug, superior disdain of the GPs. They would look down their supercilious noses at the struggling rep., and more often than not they didn't have to tell him what to do with his medical supplies! And those were the ones who agreed to see him!

It never stopped them accepting all the hand-outs and incentives, however. David's stomach would churn every time he handed over a leather-bound folder, or a Parker pen, discreetly printed with his drug company's logo. There were a lot more gifts besides. Bigger and better ones. David didn't think it was corrupt; he was just mad as hell he wasn't on the receiving end!

David spent hours on the motorways. They all looked the same. Did it matter? Did anything matter any more? Sometimes he found himself thinking about his brother, Paul. What must he have made of those strange postcards? But David just didn't have the guts to tell him anything. He had tried, after all, confiding in his father, and...

David broke out in a cold sweat, and turned off at the next service area. He couldn't bear to dwell on it any longer.

'Besides,' he thought, 'Paul has made it. Who the hell am I to drag him down because of my fucked-up life? He must be a senior partner in his advertising firm by now; he always got what he wanted, lucky bastard! He didn't want to be a doctor, and Dad didn't give *him* a hard time. He must be living in a fancy house in London, with fancy women, not a care in the world, the bastard...'

David blinked hard to try and break the destructive line of thought.

He parked the car, walked towards the building, and headed straight for the men's toilet. He splashed his face with cold water, and looked at himself in the mirror; his thin, gaunt face had a grey tinge to it. He combed his bony hand through his black hair. The hair off his face made him look even more haggard.

Taking in some deep breaths, he was ready to face the world.

It must be time for lunch. He noticed that the restaurant had a bar next door.

Sipping a glass of lager, he studied his worksheet. On it were sixteen names and addresses of doctors' surgeries in the Greater Manchester area.

That should take care of the afternoon. He ordered another lager.

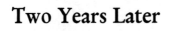

Two Years Later

Chapter Forty-Nine

Helen was sitting at the breakfast bar in her new kitchen, reading the latest House & Garden magazine. Ever since moving to the apartment in St. John's Wood, she had become obsessed with furnishings, decor, and kitchen appliances. It was never like this when she lived in the bed-sit, or when she shared with Trevor; it was amazing what a difference a mortgage could make.

The ground floor Victorian apartment was spacious and in wonderful condition, given its age.

It had been totally re-wired, along with the other apartments in the same building, and the previous owner had moved out some four months earlier, leaving the walls pure white, the floorboards bare, and a kitchen so dated Helen was convinced the oven had probably baked many a Victoria sponge – *for* Queen Victoria! But it was plain and unspoilt, like an artist's canvas; she was able to decorate room by room, exactly to her taste.

It had three good sized bedrooms, and a large, square lounge with an original Adams fireplace. The bathroom was simply stunning, and although as old as the kitchen, there was no way she wanted to update it. It had a white cast iron bath set on claw feet, and a huge, oversized Art Deco washbasin. She had replaced the shabby lace curtains with a wooden-slatted blind.

Two hardwood French doors led out onto a full-width patio edged with a little grass and a few flowers. Gardening would have to become her next hobby.

She finished her coffee and toast and stacked the cup and plate in the dishwasher. Unlike most Monday mornings, there was no rush today because she didn't have to start her shift in Accident and Emergency until eleven. She had made the most of her relaxed start to the week; a bath instead of a two minute shower, breakfast instead of a chocolate biscuit, and she had even managed to read the paper on the same day it was delivered.

Although it was a freezing cold November morning, Helen wanted to walk to the hospital today. She didn't get much exercise these days, and as long as it was dry it was a lot easier to walk to King George's than wait for a bus. She put on a big thick jacket, switched the dishwasher on, and left by the front door.

As London roads went, this one was fairly quiet. Not a lot of through traffic, but parking was still a dreadful problem. Helen walked past her shiny black Volkswagen Golf. It was more trouble than it was worth to drive to the hospital, so it usually stayed there all week, safe with a resident's permit in the windscreen, and Helen looked forward to drives in the country, and picnics, on her days off.

Block by block, the roads got busier. Red buses, black cabs and multi-coloured vans were clogging every inch of tarmac. Everyone was in a hurry. Except Helen.

She strolled past a man in white overalls who was up a ladder, pasting a new advertisement onto an enormous billboard. He was about half way done, and it was already clear what the advert was going to be; she had seen the same ad. before. Helen stopped and watched him run his long handled brush over the wet sections. She was smiling.

The advert for 'Cajun Kitchens' was very ordinary, and just like the adverts for any other fast food outlet, but Helen liked it the best.

She looked down at her wedding ring; a simple rose-gold band, not very big, but it was the one possession she was most proud of. She only wore the diamond solitaire on special occasions; with her hands in and out of surgical gloves all day long, the massive one carat diamond became a real nuisance.

She twisted the ring around her finger. It turned easily in the cold. She was still smiling to herself as she put her hands in her pockets and carried on walking. As she took one last look at the poster, she hoped no one would guess what was making her smile: rampant sex last night on the new Persian rug in front of the burning coal fire.

'Who would have thought sex with your husband could be so much fun!'

Helen walked along the crowded London streets in a world of her own. She was thinking about the time she made love in the newly fitted kitchen, sitting on top of the granite work surface. Then there was the bath. All the bedrooms. And a couple of times on the patio under the cover of darkness. The sun lounger had never been quite the same. She made a mental note to buy a new one next summer.

Wrapped in her warm thoughts she reached the hospital in no time. It was a majestic building; the old wing was original Georgian with stone pillars and ornate workings on the windows and roof eaves. The new wing was hideous, prefabricated and grey, but at least it was only partially visible from the main entrance. The accident and emergency department was in the new block. Away from the road, the only vehicles allowed in front were the ambulances. Helen crossed the access road and went up some steps to the doctors' locker room. She hoped today would be quiet; there were two steaks defrosting on the draining board, and a nice bottle of claret all ready on the dining table.

The Adams fireplace and Persian rug were beckoning.

*

"Morning, Andy. Lovely morning, isn't it?"

"No. It's bloody freezing if you ask me!" Andy was a senior hospital porter, who was nearly as old as the hospital. He was, however, in a far worse state of disrepair, and wasn't anything like as good to look at. All the doctors and nurses had a passing joke with the grumpy old man, who really was a kind hearted soul, but kept the act up, relentlessly.

Helen left Andy wheeling an old man to theatre and headed for the A & E department her crisp white coat flapping as she marched through the maze of corridors, stethoscope rolled up in her left pocket, pens, paper and assorted junk in her right.

"Morning Phil. What have we got?" Phil was the duty charge nurse, who was the nerve centre of the place. He was healer, mediator, administrator, and general nice guy. A friend and ally to both the medical staff and the dreaded management; everyone wanted to be his friend. Helen and Phil got on famously. In the early days as junior houseman, Helen had turned to Phil on numerous occasions. He had always been there for her, with a helping hand, and a friendly word. Now, they shared a mutual respect for each other.

"Hello, Helen. Very quiet, you'll be pleased to hear.

"There are a couple of possible fractures, usual array of cuts and sprains. Nothing too exciting. How's that husband of yours? Lucky sod!"

"He's fine, thanks Phil. Oh, do you and Angela fancy coming over for supper this Friday?"

"Friday. Yep, that should be okay. If there's a problem, I'll get Angela to give you a ring. Thanks."

Helen checked the next name on the list. She went out to the waiting room. There were children running about, workmen nursing various parts of their extremities, and a couple of teenage schoolgirls who looked fit and healthy but were trying hard to look sad. Always the same on Monday mornings. "Margaret Neely?" One of the schoolgirls stood up and followed Helen into a cubicle.

"Right Margaret, what's the problem?"

The girl was obviously embarrassed and regretting the fact that her teacher had given her the benefit of the doubt.

"I've got terrible stomach pains. But they're a bit better now."

"Let's have a look." The girl lay down on the bed, Helen knew her time was probably being wasted. But she gave her a thorough examination just the same. There was no inflammation or tenderness.

"Have you got your period, Margaret!"

The words might just as well have been, "You're going to die," because instantly the lanky schoolgirl burst into tears. Helen would have found it amusing, had it not been such a waste of everyone's time, money and effort. With resources stretched to the limit, it made her angry to have her days filled with time-wasters, while genuine cases had to wait. In the eighteen months that Helen had been working at King George's she must have had to attend to hundreds of so-called patients, who really could have been sorted out with a plaster, or a couple of aspirin. 'Five years of study, to stick a Band-Aid on a finger!'

She sent Margaret out to her waiting teacher with instructions that she could miss games today.

Margaret was delighted.

It was almost four o'clock when Helen stopped for a coffee. Her days always appeared to fly by. She should be home by seven thirty; plenty of time to get the dinner ready.

As she arrived back at the waiting room, a boy came through the double doors, holding a wad of tissues against his head. The white tissues were almost totally red with blood. He was about ten, wearing rugby boots, shorts and shirt. He too had a teacher in tow. After a quick scan of the waiting room, Helen was satisfied there was no one more urgent, so she called the boy out of turn.

"Oi! I've been 'ere for fuckin' hours!" A large man in workman's clothes stood up. He had taken off his left boot and sock exposing a filthy, callus-encrusted foot. Helen noticed that he seemed to by standing on it without too much pain and discomfort.

"Someone will see to you shortly. And please mind your language!" She took the boy through, while his teacher filled out his details at the reception desk. Helen removed the sodden mass of paper from the back of his head. There was a deep gash almost an inch long. The boy had stopped crying but his sobs continued. A nurse came in to offer a hand. She smiled at the little boy, instinctively trying to make him feel more relaxed.

"This nurse is one of our best. She's going to stick you up with super-glue! Is that okay?" The little boy, who gave his name as 'Rupert Middleton Hargreaves', could manage a tearful nod. "She'll give you a little injection to take the pain away, as well." Helen smiled and left Julie, the staff nurse, with the brave little public schoolboy. "Better get him up to X-ray afterwards, just in case. Thanks Julie."

Helen came out of the cubicle and bumped into Phil. He looked serious.

"Ambulance control have radioed in. There's been a nasty RTA on the flyover; five vehicles, two dead at the scene, and at least four badly injured."

"What's their ETA?"

Phil looked at his watch, "Seven minutes."

"Okay. Let's get the trauma team standing by. Page the duty casualty consultants, would you?"

"Done that already. I'll try and shift some of these people." He went out into the waiting room. The number of patients waiting to be seen had risen to about thirty. Those that decided to stay would be in for a long wait.

While the crash teams awaited the arrival of the ambulances, Helen rushed to the lavatory. She didn't know when she might next get the chance. Phil briefed the available doctors and nurses, while Andy and two other porters stood by, nervously, keeping out of the way, but ready to help at a moment's notice. It was like a well-rehearsed drill; everyone knew their roles. There was no panic, just orderly, professional activity.

Helen joined the rest of the trauma team, who had all donned plastic aprons. The curtains around the examination cubicles were pulled right back. They were checked for equipment. Everything was ready.

In the distance faint sirens could be heard above the hubbub inside the hospital. The familiar noise grew louder as the fleet of ambulances approached the hospital entrance. Helen's superior, Mr Hughes, a casualty consultant, was the first to see each injured person as they were stretchered out. With expert efficiency, he called out instructions to the waiting team of medics, and one by one the casualties were rushed to each of the prepared cubicles and examination rooms.

Helen rushed alongside her designated patient. He was male but there was so much blood obscuring his face and head it was impossible to make out anything else about him. Two paramedics from the ambulance wheeled the stretcher, all the time giving an update on their injured charge:

"Male, about thirty. He was trapped in the wreckage. When we got to him, he was fibrulating. We cardioverted him and put down an ET tube: double dose Atropine and adrenaline"

"What are his vital signs?"

"Resps: 30 per minute, pulse: 120, BP: 80 over 40."

"What's he had in the canulas?"

"Two units of Colloid and one litre of saline."

With everyone acting as one, they gently lifted the limp, battered body onto the examination bed. A nurse removed the stained ambulance blanket. His legs were in blow-up splints; white bone was poking through the torn flesh.

"Oh, yeah. Compound fractures to tibia and fibula, both legs."

"Thanks, chaps." Helen put the ends of her stethoscope into her ears and moved alongside the man. "Cross-match six units of blood, and let's have some 'O' neg. now. We've got to get him stabilised."

Simon, a senior registrar from the Orthopaedic ward had come across to assist. The paramedics, their work done, tidied up their stretcher. As they left the examination room, one of them went close to Helen, "He's been drinking."

Helen clicked her tongue, disapprovingly. "Was he driving?"

"Well, if you can call it driving. It looks like he caused the accident. What a mess!"

Helen sighed and shook her head at the needless waste of life, but got on with the job in hand, determined to try and save *this* life. It wasn't her job to judge people. Just fix them up.

All his clothes had been cut away and removed from his broken body. He was very thin, almost emaciated. Helen listened to his chest. A nurse swabbed away blood from his face and head.

"I don't think there's any major trauma to his chest. How's the blood pressure?"

"75 over 40."

"He must be bleeding internally. We've *got* to get him stabilised."

Helen glanced towards his cleaned up face.

She froze.

David O'Connor opened his eyes and looked up from the bed.

*

Helen gasped and took a step back. She looked at the injured man's face. A long hard look. There was no mistake; the man who had once made her pregnant, who wanted to marry her, who tried to kill her, was lying a couple of feet in front of her.

David O'Connor was in shock. He was staring at Helen, but he didn't see her. He couldn't have seen her. Could he?

"Doctor... Doctor! Are you alright?" The nurse who was monitoring the blood pressure noticed Helen standing quite still, frozen. Helen couldn't speak.

An on-call consultant marched into the room and walked past Helen to take up his place by the staring man's head. While he examined the man, with other members of the trauma team giving him all the facts, Helen couldn't remove her gaze from David O'Connor's blood-stained face.

The consultant removed his stethoscope from his ears. "I think we may have internal bleeding. We're going to have to open him up. Is theatre standing by?"

"Yes doctor."

*

David O'Connor was in shock. His flesh was grey and drained. His eyes carved out a path through all the people standing around him. His gaze was fixed on Helen.

Her head was telling her that there was no way a patient in severe shock could make out surroundings and recognise anyone. Her heart was telling her that he was staring straight into her eyes.

Mr Hughes, the senior casualty consultant, came in. His patient had died. He saw Helen. This was not the Helen he knew.

"Doctor. Do you want to come outside for a moment." It wasn't a question. He took a firm grip of her right elbow and marched her out, hoping the other consultant had not noticed.

He stood close by her side and marched her into the doctor's common room. He closed the door and turned the rod of the blinds to give them some privacy.

"What the *Hell* do you think you're playing at?" He was more worried for Helen than angry, but that didn't make him shout any less. Helen gazed into space. He had never seen her like this. "Helen!" He shook her by the arms. She was jolted out of her trance.

Finally, almost in a whisper, she spoke, "I know him."

"Who? The patient in Resus.? Are you sure?"

"Yes. I'm positive." She looked at Mr Hughes. "He's my brother-in-law."

Chapter Fifty

David O'Connor was cremated on a freezing cold November morning.

Having suffered a ruptured spleen in the accident he had died before reaching the operating theatre. He was twenty-eight.

Paul and Helen O'Connor were the only people at his funeral. His mother sent flowers, but she wasn't able to fly home from New Zealand. She and her husband, Tom, were playing in a bridge tournament that weekend. At least she sent flowers.

Paul wrapped his arm around his wife as they left the crematorium. They had both done a lot of crying over the last few days, but they didn't cry now. It was too late for that.

The drive back to St. John's Wood was in silence. Paul nervously tapped his wedding ring against the steering wheel. He parked the Golf a short way from their home. Helen got out and linked arms with her husband as they walked.

As he opened the front door, the phone began to ring. Helen answered it. "Hello?"

"Hi. This is Matt calling from New York. Is Paul there?"

"Just a minute..." She covered the mouthpiece and called out to him in the kitchen. "...Paul, it's that creep from your New York office. Do you want to talk to him?"

Paul came out of the kitchen eating an apple. He nodded and took the phone. "Matt! Hi! Listen, I'm not going into the office for a couple of days, the advertising world will just have to do without me for a while! My brother has died, and we've just come home from his funeral, so excuse me if I can't get enthusiastic about an ad campaign for some, 'Chicken..Gumbo..Kitchens' right now!"

"Cajun Kitchen."

"Whatever! That *is* what you were calling me about, isn't it?... I thought so. Look, give Tony a call. He knows as much about it as I do. I'm sorry, Matt, you've caught me at a bad time."

He put the receiver back. Helen went over to him and put her arms around his waist. This was the man who normally would eat, breathe, and sleep advertising, but not today.

They hugged each other. "I'm so lucky to have you, Hel. Just think, if David hadn't gone missing, I wouldn't have come to see you. I wouldn't have asked you out. I wouldn't have fallen in love with you. We owe so much to David!"

Helen had never told him about Atlantic Beach, and what really happened out there. She certainly wasn't about to burst his bubble now.

"Are you sure you shouldn't go to work, take your mind off things?" She really wanted him here, all to herself, but she knew what a workaholic he could be.

"No. It'll do me good to have a couple of days off. If the boss can't take time off when he likes, why be the boss? Anyhow, I only had one important meeting tomorrow, and Tony can sit in." Slowly, Paul began to smile. "Maybe you should take the meeting tomorrow!"

"*Me*? What do I know about advertising?"

"It's with a top man from this new American fast food chain we've been working on. He's in London right now. I've met him a couple of times. The girls in the office go crazy when he walks in; say he looks like a film star. Maybe he'll put you under his spell! I think he looks like a complete prat!

"...But, the campaign is worth a fortune! You could soften him up for me. Actually, that's not a bad idea; he could come round here for dinner! Yeah! These Yanks love the personal touch!"

Helen had had her suspicions ever since Cajun Kitchens started to pop up in London. What she had now was far too special to even think about rocking the boat. She never asked what the man's name was, but how many 'film stars' could one restaurant chain employ? It *had* to be him. And she didn't want to know!

"Paul. I love you dearly, as you know. But I am a doctor. You are in advertising. I won't bring any of my patients home, if you won't bring any of your clients home. Deal?" She was smiling trying to keep it light-hearted, but she needed the message to get home.

"Okay, deal."

They kissed and then Helen took a bite out of his apple. "Oi!" He started to jokingly grab her, she wriggled free.

"No. Don't! I have to go to the loo."

"God! I don't believe it! Not again!"

Helen stopped in the doorway, thinking she better offer an explanation. "Remind me in the morning to get in touch with the Nanny Agency. Will you?"

"But I thought we'd done all that? The baby's not due for another six months."

"I know... but I want to see how they feel about looking after twins."

All Helen heard as she went into the bathroom, smiling, was a half-eaten apple falling onto the wood floor.